I0553264

Vinte's Claim

Her Enlightenment

R.F. Thelwell

VINTE'S CLAIM. Copyright © 2023. R.F. Thelwell.

All rights reserved. No portion of this book may be reproduced, stored in a retrieval system, or transmitted in any form or by any means – electronic, mechanical, photocopy, recording, scanning or other – except for a brief quotation in critical reviews or articles, without the prior written permission of the publisher or author.

Published by:

ISBN: 978-1-958404-35-5 (paperback)

This novel is a work of fiction. Names, characters, places, and incidents are either products of the author's imagination or used fictitiously. All characters are fictional, and any similarity to people living or dead is purely coincidental or maybe prophetic.

Table of Contents

Chapter 1
Terriana

I cannot believe I just fucked him. Shit.shit.shit. I swore I wouldn't, but no self-control strikes again. Seriously. Terri, you had a perfectly good pro-con list, for God's sake. He.was.not.the.one.

3 Months Earlier

Having no roommates to fuss with and no siblings to bounce ideas off is the price of living alone. As I stretched my muscles out on my king-sized bed and looked around my room, my loneliness subsided, and a sense of pride washed over me. A cascade of sunrays blinded me, seeping through my floor-to-ceiling windows—windows that also opened up my bedroom and allowed a nice contrast to my dark grey walls. Black glass furniture for a modern allure, with a soulful elegance being set by my favorite inspirational quotes on the walls with twinkling lights, yes, blue ones. Plants situated for a fresh air feel, and plush blue rugs for a homey ambiance. Home sweet home.

5

As I sat forward, I felt energized, so I pushed the sheets aside and plopped my feet in my bedside sandals, made the bed, then headed for my bathroom. Unlike my room, which smelt of fresh ocean air, my bathroom smelt of shea butter and lavender; the scent being so appealing. After warming the shower and doing my morning business, I did my hair in a neat ponytail to the back and moved over to my closet. I had so many nameless brands that gave me this chic confidence to dominate. I was never rich growing up, so now that I lived comfortably, I took pride in helping the little guy.

Today I got styled in a pink cotton dress that hugged my body and fell just below my knees with a slit at the back, stylish belt around my little waist, and a cross button cut just showing a small amount of cleavage. I accessorized with a watch on one wrist, a bracelet on the other, earrings to match, and light natural-looking makeup with pink cotton lipstick.

I felt nostalgic. Not so long ago I was homeless with no idea where my next meal would come from. Five years ago to be exact. I was fifteen, thin, with pale honeydew skin and light frizzy hair down my back. Now, I jumped in my jeans, with moisturized healthy hair and a fully stocked refrigerator. As if on queue, my stomach grumbled, propelling me to my favourite place, *my kitchen*. I briskly made breakfast. As I glanced at the

6

refrigerator magnet on my to-do list, I took account of the time: 6:45 am.

I wrapped up with breakfast and made haste to the door, grabbing my handbag and locking up on my way to the garage. Yes, I owned a car now: Mercedes Benz C Class to be exact, my baby on wheels. It took me fifteen minutes to get out of the house, into my car, and onto the freeway. Traffic had me in my parking space by 7:05 am. I closed up my car and headed next-door of my office building. Like every morning for the past five years, I got my order premade so I could be in and out of the coffee shop in five minutes. *And, no, I did not drink coffee.* I drank tea, hot bubbly and chocolatey.

This coffee shop would feed and shelter me from the rain when all else had turned their backs on me. Therefore, I returned the favour every day; *don't bite the hand that fed you, right?* The owner would kill me anyways; after all, they only made tea for me. As I opened the door and walked inside, at one glance, I was stuck in my tracks, my body went numb. I felt the blood drain from my face. From outside, the shop looked so normal, but my spidey-senses failed me today. *Big time.*

Before me stood a guy, one hand slightly raised and a triangle tattoo on the back of his neck barely visible as a result of his all-black attire and a mask of some kind

7

covering his head meeting his hairline. *Yes, his tight ass was turned to me.* Before him sat the morning employees, all three had bloodshot tear-stained eyes. All lined out before the masked guy on bended knees facing me, shaking, and disoriented. It wouldn't take a rocket scientist to tell they were manhandled and physically assaulted.

To my left were four of the regular lawyers, faced down on their cashmere custom-made suits. There were three therapists that I recognized to my right huddled together, hands bound, sitting before the donut stand with eyes panicked and fearful. This coffee shop was in a strategically placed part of town, surrounded by fortune 500 companies; banks and billionaire businesses made this shop filled with the richest and brightest customers.

As if I was in a slow trance, the door swung closed, signaling to everyone who was so fixed on the muscular, 6' something, broad shoulder man standing before me that I had indeed arrived with a ding of the doorbell. As his muscles flexed, he whipped his head around swiftly, and just like that, my knees went weak, my mouth got dry, and I was shamelessly lost in the most mesmerizing deep blue eyes I had ever seen glaring right at me. His eyes twitched for a millisecond and that sense of cloud nine drifted to psychotic fear; then I felt strong arms submerge me from behind.

8

"Bitch, on the ground. Pass me the bag."

His voice was strained as if what he was saying just didn't sit right with him. Almost forceful.

"Okay, okay. Ple-e-ease don't hurt me."

I choked out, as fear transcended to replace the numbness in my body. As I was pushed down on my knees, the strong arms that were behind me grabbed my bag. I heard shuffling and, like a switch was flipped, his aftershave had my lady parts tingling, something that had never happened to me before. *What the hell is going on?* He stretched his arm over me and picked up my cell that I didn't even realize had fallen. As I turned to look who "strong, tall, and demanding" was, his voice boomed around the room, sending a pleasurable shiver down my spine.

"Don't you dare. Face on the ground."

As if shell-shocked, I froze, eyes locked on the beautiful specimen of a man before me. I gulped, shocked speechless. I saw defined jawlines, hazel eyes with long lashes, and absolutely gorgeous lips being faded behind a stocking as a mask. *Shocking, right? This place was being robbed by supermodels.* His muscles tensed as he stared up at me with a hint of wonder that quickly turned into rage. His arm shot up towards my face and I instinctively covered my face as a breeze passed swiftly by the back of

9

my fingers. I heard a smack-like hit meet a surface, but I didn't feel it. I slowly looked up to find icy blue eyes and raging hazel eyes giving each other death stares hand in hand at my jaw. More so, icy eyes' wrist in a vice grip in hazel eyes' hand.

"What the fuck, man? Is it amateur night? She's seen your bloody face with that shitty mask," Icy blue eyes proclaimed, exasperatedly.

I looked down immediately as my senses came rushing back to me. If I had seen his face, he may want to kill me. I began to shake and whimper. "Please don't kill me. I won't tell a soul," I whispered pleadingly.

"No one's dying today, love. We just want what we came for and we'll be on our way, right?" Hazel eyes proclaimed suggestively.

With my head down, not daring to look up, I was not sure who he was talking to. *Bang!* I squeezed my eyes tighter together as if they weren't closed already. I felt my heart pounding behind my ribcage as if begging for release. As the echo evaded the room, I began to feel a rise in tension. I didn't dare to look up off the ground again. There was shuffling and muffled cries.

"Where is it, you damn dick?" Icy blue eyes sounded agitated as if running out of patience.

10

"I don't know what you want, man. I'm just a lawyer." I heard someone choke out in fear.

"God damn it, you're about to be dead, mate."

"Got it," Hazel eyes cut off icy blue eyes mid tantrum.

"Let's get the fuck out of here, now!" Icy blue eyes bellowed out, to whom I was not sure.

Were there only two of them? I heard heavy foot movements coming my way. I opened my eyes slightly, not taking them off the ground. I was now facing the door I came through. I peeped out onto the ground, six sets of feet passed me going out of the café.

One set of feet caught my attention amongst the lot. He had on combat shoes, the ones with the hidden knife compartment. My mind immediately drifted to my mom who was in the navy; she had a pair. I peeked up higher than before, the doors in mid-swing and I could see him. Broad shoulders, jet black hair, 6'4, and an infinity tattoo on his left inner wrist. As if he felt my eyes on him, he turned my way. I blinked up to see a cocky grin on his side profile as if God was saying, *Stop trying to die.*

Bang!

The door closed and the room erupted in cries of *"Are they gone?" "Are you okay?" "You're bleeding." "Put an ice pack on your jaw." "Call the office now and tell them security*

11

breach code seven." Screams of panic and footsteps. The wind was suddenly knocked out of me as someone pushed me out of their way and I went head first into the bloody door.

Then darkness covered me.

Chapter 2
Vinte

Her eyes seemed to haunt me from the moment the door closed. Big, brown, and currently glossy. Long lashes that touched her cheeks when they closed, and her skin, golden, some would say sun-kissed. Her friends called her Terri. *Yes, I cased the place, and she was a regular from the private offices next door.* The auburn brunette is 5'3 with the cutest smile and a face that can pass for a 15-year-old, even though she was 20. *Sigh, Terriana Kahaylia Watson. Yes, I ran a background check too.* I was curious about the petite modelesque. *No, it's not stalking. I should know.*

As we turned the corner onto the freeway, I felt as if something was just not right. While sitting in the jeep with my CI and his boss speeding away from the crime I aided them in committing, *undercover, of course. 'Get the list of inmates that are running drug deals on the outside along with the names of the corrupt cops and prison guards on their payroll.'* That was my mission. My CI mission was "Get the list so that this new drug connect asshat Jason can out pay these cops into 'accidentally' killing

13

their current boss" so he can be the new king of the human trafficking and drug scene.

I pulled my phone out to see if I could get an update on the people we just roughed up. Okay, so really, I was checking to see that she was okay, *sigh. She almost blew my whole cover in a flash.* Three women got bitch-slapped, a man got a fist to the face, and one of the lawyers of those imprisoned drug dealers had a broken wrist and a bullet in his leg. All by the hands of an impatient son-of-a-bitch, *asshat.*

When I told her "Bitch, on the ground, pass me the bag," I almost choked on my own tongue trying to keep my character in check. *She looked so fragile.* I couldn't let her get the same treatment as everyone else. Her face would be bruised, and I couldn't kill this asshat just yet; this bust could save thousands, all for one girl, *my girl.*

Then she had to speak, "Okay, okay, ple-e-ease don't hurt me." The voice of an angel I tell you. I had never officially met her. She had never seen me before, so when she spoke, my dick twitched immediately. *Shiiit.* I was in the middle of a robbery and I was trying to picture her saying those words to me when I was balls-deep inside her. *Sadistic, I know.*

As I pushed her down on her knees, I grabbed her bag just to make it look like a regular robbery as instructed by

14

these cowards I was babysitting. *Pushing her forward was my undoing.* The image of her on all fours bent over and her perky ass out, *I groaned in my throat.* Those pink lips had me adjusting myself. As I got really close trying to hide my boner, her body tensed. She was so responsive, and I hadn't even touched her yet. I stretched over her just to get a whiff of her intoxicating sweet scent. It was like lavender mixed with something else, something heavenly. I picked up her cell and dropped it back in her purse, *discreetly*. As she was about to turn, I saw Jason, *the asshat,* who I had to endure, looking back at us. I needed a distraction and quick.

As if she had read my mind, she began to turn around towards me. "Don't you dare. Face on the ground." I proclaimed. Her body didn't tense this time. Mid turn, her eyes locked on mine, and she swallowed. *I went numb.* Before I could fully grasp the situation, I saw Jason's hand coming down fast to slap *MY GIRL!* Not today, Satan, undercover or not. I snatched his hand in mid-air right beside her cheek. I mentally face-palmed myself, but...

"HAYY!" Asshat Jason shouted to me in the rear-view.

I jerked a little, shutting off my mental rant. "What!" I barked back.

"Did you hear what I said?" he barked agitatedly.

15

"Naah," I replied nonchalantly.

"What the fuck am I paying you for? Daydreaming or doing what I fucking say?" This arrogant piece of shit; I *cannot wait to bury him.*

Chapter 3
Terriana

The next thing I knew, I felt uncomfortable, a cloth-like material wrapped around me, a surging pain in my head. I felt the sun as it stung my exposed skin. I tried to open my eyes, but they felt heavy and tired. Faint chatter from a distance had my head gently tipped in the direction of the unfamiliar voices. I mustered up some strength and tore my eyelids open. The room was bright, and I only got a glimpse of someone's back profile speaking to a lady in white, *a doctor.*

"I can't say much because it's doctor-patient confidentiality, but her body appears to be in an induced state of panic. She appears to have a huge phobia against either the hospital or machines, so she freaked out when she woke up under the MRI machine. We had her heavily sedated, allowing her body time to stabilize."

I dosed off again.

Three days after the robbery, I woke up in a lonely hospital room with a groggy memory and a sore neck. Apparently, I didn't only have bad timing, but I was a complete head case. According to the doctors, I woke up when I was being scanned for internal bleeding and I hit my head again and ruined some of the fresh stitches from my first collision. Just my luck, right? *It got worse.* After they patched me up, they also had to do a CT scan. I freaked out again, so they had to sedate me. *I'm not crazy or anything* but when you were homeless, you get a little hysterical waking up to unfamiliar surroundings. Why do you think babies cry so often? Imagine falling asleep in your crib and waking up in a grocery store with lots of strangers giving you googly eyes, woo-ing and aw-ing. *A nightmare in a trolley, but that wasn't the worst part.*

After being cleared for visitors, *not that I would have any*, the police walked in. Armed and serious, I evaded the police for as long as I could remember. Like when I was thirteen and had to drive my dad to the hospital when I thought he was dead. *Turned out he was just tired and slept like the dead.* Being in this part of the city was my safe haven; too rich for a ticket, you barely see any cops patrolling. After all, this is the city of trust-fund kids and family legacies. You barely see anyone like me, *lawyerless.*

I could barely give a statement because my memory of the day was no longer fresh in my mind. However, I did what I could. Combat boots, tattoo, blue or hazel eyes, I was not sure. British accents, supermodel physique, and pretty tall, over six feet. I naturally have an

18

eye for detail and that was why I painted every chance I got, and how I quickly became one of the east coast's best psychologists in five years; *I read people.* The cops said that based off my position in the incident, they expected me to have more details, as if they were fishing to bring up all my memories.

They left with disappointed looks and said they would be 'in touch' if they needed any more information. Not that I was hoping to be needed or anything. *Who wants witness protection* and gangsters looking for them? When the nurses arrived shortly after with discharge papers, I was reluctantly eager to get the hell up out of there. They asked for an emergency contact and asked who would be collecting me. I think they realised I had no one and had pity on me when I shifted uncomfortably in the bed. I could have written Jess' info, *but I didn't want her to worry.* They sat down the papers and gave me privacy. I didn't wait for them to return. I got changed in my dress and out of the hospital gown, signed up the paperwork, gathered my things and stumbled around until I found my way outside.

The strangest thing happened when I got out. I saw my baby as my feet hit the asphalt. My Merci in all her glory, sleek black doors, tinted glass, blue headlights with custom rims, leather seats and customized interior lighting, *done by yours truly,* sitting in the parking space

19

smack across from the entrance. *I gave myself a mini orgasm just looking at her.* How did she get here was question two on my mind. Question one was, how did God know I needed her? As I raced across the parking space to my car, I started to feel self-conscious. Here I was running with a meerkat smile out of a hospital with my hair disheveled, my clothes cute but stained with blood, and an expensive handbag swinging towards an expensive car, with six-hundred-dollar heels tapping away.

I must have looked like a looney thief, and then again, there was the issue of being black while running to make matters worse. I looked like a thin Madea. I started rummaging in my handbag and pulled out my keys, *peep peep.* I heard footsteps approaching so I slid quickly into my seat, closed and locked my door. When I looked up there was no one there. *Well, no one looking in my direction;* pure paranoia. *Shake it off, girlfriend.* Keys in the ignition, and I was off.

After fleeing the hospital, I spent the rest of the day at home to get my bearings in check, then resumed my regular routine. I would have avoided the coffee shop for a while, but my only friend, Jessica, showed up at my apartment at 2 am the next morning. Well, *she had a key*, so it was more like her storming into my bedroom after relieving her thirst in the kitchen with my 'good' wine.

"Why did you leave the hospital alone? I was going to pick you up, Terri. You could have re-injured yourself," she said, waltzing in, scaring me out of my light slumber.

I sat up and blinked a couple of times before adjusting to the darkness. "I was fine, and besides, Merci was right out front," I said staring at her like the crazy she was.

"Who brought your car there?" she asked puzzled.

"I thought you did it." I really didn't think it was her. I just didn't want to say what I think, *because it was crazy.* Nothing was missing; it was all in one piece, and I had the keys in my purse at the hospital.

"No, I didn't make it to the city until two hours ago. You were supposed to still be in the hospital for my visit, until tomorrow," she said, giving me that 'You're in big trouble missy' stare down.

"You know I hate that place. Dead and sick people are two things I hate the most," I said, laying down and giving her my back. I heard her sigh and some shuffling. I guess she was raiding my closet again, then the bed dips. I didn't have a guest room. The apartment was expensive enough, so when she was here, she was in my bed.

A week later, I woke up super early and took a run while Jess slept soundly, probably still jetlagged from her trip a week ago.

21

Vinte's Claim

Lazy bones.

I met Jessica five years ago when this better version of myself was born. She inherited the coffee shop space from her grandpa with a lot of cash when she was fourteen. Her family wasn't the regular picture-perfect family just like mine. She was rebellious, expressive, and she didn't take shit from no one. So, when her mom believed her stepdad over her all the time, she withdrew from them mentally. Just because you marry into wealth to maintain your own wealth, that doesn't mean common sense was married in.

Eventually, she hid and got her GED, and started the café at only sixteen with her aunt helping her. When I met Jess, she was a year in the business and the shop was a success. Pearrie J Café was named after her grandpa who obviously knew she would need her inheritance young and that she could handle the responsibilities of the money entrusted to her. She was making money from the cafe enough to enroll in college, and her mom allowed it with her own hidden agenda that did not last very long. Her mom kicked Jess out the minute she stopped paying her stepfather's bail money every few weeks. So, she fixed the upstairs loft space that she wasn't using and turned it into her apartment. The day after she moved in was the day my life changed for the better. We met when she almost tripped over me sleeping at the foot of her cafe

22

doorway downstairs, when she was about to go run around the block.

I slept on her steps every day that year until she caught me. *It was fate.* When one door closes, another opens, right? She took me in, gave me a job and a fresh out-of-the-store couch. Eventually, she had me doing classes online with her and got me an internship in psychology with her aunt until I made something of myself. Five years later, she was the big sister I dreamt of.

My mom was in the navy and died on duty somewhere around the world. We never got a body, only a flag on an empty coffin. My dad handled his emotions as best as he could. After the funeral service and all the friends and little family left, *he changed.* The light in his eyes turned right off like a faucet—drunk before noon and dead asleep by five.

I was eleven when mom passed. I was fourteen when my dad showed up with a woman on his arm engaged. How does a drunk get engaged? How does a drunk get married and move away when his daughter was at school? When you are fifteen, and you have pawned away all that was left in the house that was once a home and social services showed up at the door, what do you do? *You run, that's what.*

My dad was a gentle soul when I was growing up. He was the constant out of both parents with my mom having to leave all the time. He taught me all my life skills. We did all my firsts together; first time riding a bicycle, driving a car, fixing cars, how to read people's behavior, how to be invisible in a crowd. Weird stuff, now that I think about it, but he would make them into games so they were always fun and had me laughing from ear to ear when I was small. He would call me his Bluebell because I once dyed my hair blue by accident. He was always the quietest one in the house, always busy fixing something, adjusting something, or fixed on the computer using zeros and ones doing maths. All in all, I never imagined he would abandon me the way he did.

Mom taught me dangerous stuff for my age, so deep down I think I knew the navy would have taken her some day. Who taught their seven-year-old how to fire and reload guns? Who taught an eight-year-old how to hot wire a car? Who taught a nine-year-old how to hold her breath underwater for an abnormal amount of time? I never told my dad about what mom and I would disappear and do whenever she was home. I guess I always knew it wasn't right but wanted to bond with her by any means. She would tell me stories about her adventures

24

and make me promise to take them to the grave. Being so young, I treasured those memories; they were all I lived for when my world came crashing down.

As the sweat dripped down my face, between my breast, and down my back, I felt a little lightheaded. My body was mildly shaking, my breathing was restricted, *choked*. My chest rapidly rose and fell, pushing my hardened nipples up and down, while my lips were in a pout and my throat as dry as the Sahara Desert. I licked my lips; I was bent forward with my hair dangling down sticking to the sides of my flushed face, my hands on my thighs, knees bent, and my legs spread. "Why do you insist on overdoing your morning run like that? You keep giving yourself mini panic attacks, Terri," Jess proclaimed.

"I keep having flashbacks when I run is all. Sorry," I heaved, calming myself and shook my head. I had flashbacks running for as long as I could remember, but I never told her. I glanced up and saw her in my kitchen on the bar stool, coffee in hand. I didn't know how she drank that crap.

I made my way to the kitchen from my spot at the front door. I grabbed a mug from the cupboard and fixed myself some tea ignoring the 'please elaborate' look Jess was giving me. I listened to people's problems and gave them coping advice for a living. If I needed a therapist, I had colleagues for that. She had enough to worry about after all.

"Let's go out tonight," I said a little out of the blue or to change the topic.

"You? Go out? Ha. If you don't want to tell me, you could have chosen a better deflector, Terri." Jess said with a little sigh she thought I missed.

"I'm serious. Let's act our age for a little tonight," I said with a bite to my lip and a pleading look.

She smirked at me, took her mug to her head, and emptied it. "Okay, let's do it, but ground rules. No sleeping, no reading a book in a corner, and I'm taking you shopping for a slutty dress," Jess said with a 'please try me' look on her face.

I might be a bit of an introvert, while my friend was a huge social butterfly. I gulped before nodding yes and taking my mug to my head. When I was through, I looked up at her and opened my mouth to speak and she glared at me. Yes, lips closed immediately. *Sigh. What had I gotten myself into!*

After arguing about paying for my shoes after Jess locked me in a changing room while she paid for my

26

dress, a manicure and pedicure, and a Brazilian wax later, we were at her loft getting ready to go to some upscale club near the café. Jessica was a natural knockout; milky white skin, long legs, black wavy hair to her waist, hourglass physique with just enough melons in front and behind to make any man stop and stare. So, when she styled herself in black Louboutin heels, black ripped skinny jeans with her belly ring out, and a red bustier to match her lips, you know we were in for trouble. I, on the other hand, tried to play it safe but was outvoted or bullied, *either way*. Hence, I had on a pair of six-inch heels, with stripe short shorts, a crop top with a matching cute blazer, paired with long drop earrings and a thigh chain. Our makeup was on point, thanks to Jess. We looked dangerously good.

Finding the club was easy. Jess had been there a couple of times. *'Rich' people unwinding, I guess.* Jess wasn't your typical trust-fund business owner. She didn't have an ego like the rest, and she was selfless along with fierce in a protective way. Sometimes I forgot she could afford to shop without fear. She didn't need to work, *but we loved having a purpose.* So, when we got to the club, we simply joined the line. When we were like six persons away from the door, the big hulky guy manning the door started to stare at me and eye-fuck Jess.

Apparently, the big, scary-looking softy had told Jess not to wait in line on several occasions. We trotted inside and took a quick look around, heading straight for the bar; liquid courage always did the trick. Two shots and five rejected dance offers in, and I was ready to call it a night. As if she was reading my mind, or my bored face, she grabbed me by the wrist, placed my jacket down, then aimed for the dance floor. Before I could protest, my song chimed in and I got a little excited. Before I knew it, I was moving to the rhythm with my hips swinging and my hands in the air.

I got so lost swaying and singing to the song that I hadn't noticed strong arms wrap around me from behind. With his large hands firmly on my hips, my song blaring, and the alcohol finally giving a buzz, I got a little out of character and pushed back on him just *a little*. I didn't want to give the wrong impression; after all, we were just dancing. He had rhythm, and I could feel him getting excited; that or he had an umbrella separating us. Our hips were in synced, and his hands ran the length from my hips to my thigh chain and back up again. The music shifted from my song to another more seductive.

At this point our bodies were feverish. His fingers were digging into my thighs as he caressed me. It did hurt, it felt...really good. There was a knot building in the pit of my stomach. He removed one hand, and I instantly

28

missed the sudden loss of contact, but it was appeased when he oh so lightly pulled my hair behind my ear and pushed it over the opposite shoulder. My neck was on full display. His breath-fanned my neck and moved north to my ear. He planted a kiss behind my ear, and *I lost it.* I moaned with delight, praying the music drowned out the sound as he lightly stroked my neck with the small beds of his fingers. It was a blessing he couldn't see the effect that small gesture had on me. This sea of intoxicated intertwined bodies in the dark almost seemed nonexistent at that moment.

"Are you always this stunning, even in the dark, gorgeous?" He whispered directly into my ear, tickling my senses further, *instantly damp*. His voice was manly with a mixed accent. *Seductive.* The breath on my neck as light as a feather was all it took; traitorous body I tell you. My body had an impulsive mind of its own. I realised I was yet to respond while I let this stranger plant kisses on my neck.

"Mhm. I am, I...shit," I whispered completely out of breath like the wind was knocked out of me. What was he doing to me? *Was I drunk?* Then as if I wasn't on the brink of giving him everything he wanted and more, his thumb began rubbing delicate circles on my hip that he held firmly in place. For good measure, I presume, my knees gave way ages ago, along with my powers of

29

restraint and self-dignity no less. *We're in the middle of the dance floor!* As if I wasn't already powerless, I felt his hand creeping up my thighs, *Lord.* This man had me tongue-tied and I hadn't even seen his lips yet, so I did just that. I turned. *As if Rihanna and Drake had made a baby,* realization daunted on me that I had just made the biggest mistake that night. The face that launched a thousand ships no longer belonged to Daenerys from Game of Thrones.

The most gorgeous pair of hazel eyes with full lips, well-defined jawline, and freshly groom beard ogled me, a completely desirous look. *The feeling is mutual, sir.* All this time we were swaying and my brain failed to register the mixture of spices and the whiff of the most heavenly cologne, both opening up my nostrils and lips. My body then committed the most heinous of acts. I froze completely, because the cat got my tongue real good. I stopped swaying, my eyes were locked. Lips in a pout and heart beating greedily.

He looked like a Greek god, black button up with the two top buttons opened, sleeves rolled up to his elbows, *yes*, black slacks, dress shoes, gold watch, and cup links. He had style, no doubt about it, and he knew his presence was affecting me. I mentally face-palmed myself for openly checking him out. "Like what you see, love?"

30

Damn it. Perfect teeth, white and sexy. He smirked at me, and I got the strangest feeling. You know the feeling you get when you've done something before or seen something done before, *I don't know*. Déjà vu, I suppose, but when? I internally shook my head. No way I could have met him and forgotten, *impossible.*

"May I buy you a drink?" Why did I just say that? That was his line. Darn it. I offended him.

If the little puzzled look on his face wasn't an indication, what he said next definitely was. "I would be lying if I said that a beautiful woman had ever bought me a drink. That's definitely my role."

Subtly telling me no, I presumed. I glanced down a little worried he was regretting approaching me at all. *I'm a fish out of water here.*

"Since you're absolutely breath-taking, I'll accept the offer. Just so you know, next time will be on me, princess."

Did he say next time?

I squinted instantaneously with a little giddy smile, like a little schoolgirl. He grinned from ear to ear at my reaction, then his eyes shifted focus to something else, something that had his smile dropping like the Big Ben. It was written as plain as day on this dimly lit dance floor that he was worried. His grip on my hip even tightened.

31

"It seems like I will be finding you in a short while. You and your friend need to leave the club immediately and go straight home," He whispered—yelled—in my ear for the first time tonight.

I tried taking a glimpse behind me, but he held me firmly braced up on him. This promptly knocked me out of the haze I was locked in. Still trapped in his arms, I squared my shoulders. There were two things I hated: being told what to do and when to do it.

"Excuse me?" I am a grown woman, inexperienced, but I own an apartment and a Mercedes for peace's sake. *Is this what they term clubbing: caress a girl like you're interested, then drop her like a hot potato?*

"Hey?" He whisper yelled again. "Get your friend and get going now, gorgeous. Some very bad people just walked in. I'll come find you."

Even though his voice had a hundred percent finality in it, '*don't try me'* tone, I still tried him. "What if you're the very bad person?" With that said, I walked away from him with an apologetic look on his face. I didn't know what to think or why I said that. I thought we were having a good time or was I reading it all wrong?

After making my way to the bar, I scanned my peripherals for Jess. Anyone could spot Jess from a mile away. Just look for the string of broken pride and hearts

32

she'd left in her wake. I grabbed her hand and told her we were leaving. "No, it's too early. What happened with the sex god you were grinding on?"

I tensed and knew my face was as red as a tomato. "I was not grinding on him," I shrieked.

She folded her arms and glared at me with a "bitch, please" look. I rolled my eyes and grabbed her arm, tugging her behind me. She looked bored with the guys we stepped away from, so I knew I was saving her in hindsight.

Not even two steps away from the scary-looking security guard shamelessly checking out Jess, explosions frightened me with the music abruptly inaudible. More explosions erupted having everyone in a frenzy.

Bang! Bang! Bang! Bang!

33

Chapter 4
Vinte

Being a young detective was literally all I ever wanted to be. I was thirteen when I first saved someone. She was beaten to a bloody pulp, and her arm was broken in three places. The sad part was, her husband's response to being caught was "She shouldn't have gone through my phone."

Being an athlete and being raised right taught me a couple of things growing up. One was never to put your hands on a woman because your hit is deadly and they're fragile. The second lesson, make your own decisions. It was your life to live and your right to live. So, I called the police on my stepdad for my mom's right to live, despite his pleas at first, which turned to rage later. The police showed up with my mom weak from screaming and from her battered body and with my biceps wrapped around my stepdad's throat in a vice grip.

I got enlisted in the army when I was eighteen. I did one term, which lasted four years of my life. Then I became a cop at twenty-two when I wanted something more than war. After a year, I got promoted to a detective based on my military abilities. Now here I was, playing this final part of this cover that suffocated three months of my life. Tonight was the night I got to either shoot this asshat—*please give me a reason*—or throw him in a deep hole in prison along with some others. This club was a little too crowded for me, but it was where Jason kidnapped his girls by getting them high off their asses, and no one batted an eye when a guy walked off with a pretty rich girl stumbling around. We wanted him on all charges, and this was the final nail in the coffin; catch him in the act and all. My job tonight was to make sure that I was the guy to snatch tonight's girl. I already had my partner in position, being the perfect bait. She fitted his MO; doe eye and pretty with daddy's black card, well, the precincts card.

Imagine my surprise when I spotted *my girl* in the most teasing outfit I had ever seen. Her skin was like gold, smooth and shimmery, waist-length hair like a phoenix, and her eyes, *damn*, deep brown and calling for me. My feet took its own accord and moved a little closer to her. Her face looked like when the sun joined the ocean on the horizon. *Unequivocally breath-taking.* As I drank her in from head to toe, I felt truly appreciative of the glorious work God imploded on her. Her hair was straight, and it fell to her waist. Her little booty shorts fell right below her round ass and got an extra praise from my dick with

36

each sway. One of her thighs glistened with each movement. Body jewelry, *how sexy*, paired with her fuck-me-boots are everything. *God, give me strength*. I couldn't make out her nipples, but she had no bra on. The swell of her breast were calling for my lips. She looked succulent as ever.

I looked around and saw everyone in incognito waiting for the asshat to arrive. It was as if they didn't see her. *Was I dreaming her right now*? I needed to dream her up a darn jacket to cover up. "ETA?" I discreetly whispered into my mic. My boss responded thirty minutes out that we should just mingle. *Don't have to tell me twice*. The closer I got to her at the bar, the more I realized she needed to get out of there; shit was about to get real, and I couldn't have her mixed up in all that. So I did what I was told to do for once. I played it safe and mingled into the crowd.

As I was about to reach out to her, her friend pulled her onto the dance floor. At first, I studied her. This was her song, it appeared. Her whole mood just transformed. I gradually approached her like a lion approaching his prey, and boy was I hungry for this kill. As my fingers glided over her lower back and settled on her hips perfectly, I felt her body tense, then slowly relaxed into me.

I came alive, wrapped around her. I matched her rhythm, and her body was perfectly affixed to mine, like she was made for me. I couldn't help the murderous smile I had on daring anyone to try and cut in. Her friend even came over to check on her. She was so lost in my arms. I don't believe she even realized. My fingers roamed her hips down and back up repeatedly. I could feel a warm sensation that was building between us. As the music blared, it was like we were the only ones there. I moved my hands further up and I could feel her body's reaction. She was flustered, angry even. I pulled her hair over her ear and out of my way. The gold earring she was wearing made her ear look sexy. How can one's ear look sexy? *I had it bad.*

I planted one kiss behind her ear and trailed my finger down her neckline. Her skin was so soft, and she smelt delicious. A hint of lavender and something I couldn't place for the life of me. I lingered on her neck with my lips, dropping light kisses of appreciation. I knew she wasn't the kind of woman to let strangers touch her as feverishly as I was, but so help me God, I couldn't get enough of her. Plus, the sweet little mood that she appeared to be in was all the encouragement I needed. Then, as if I was already captivated by her, she released a little moan; *so responsive.* Definitely my cue to apply a little more pressure. I wanted her writhing in my arms.

As if reading my mind, she did just that, like her body was on fire, her hips began grinding hard against my cock, as if it wasn't already throbbing from the restraint of my slacks.

The room was dark but the small neon lights illuminated her face marvelously, and I was loving how flushed her face appeared all because of me. Then she did it again. *Damn it.* "Are you always this stunning, even in the dark, gorgeous?" She heard me, but she appeared to be on a high, too far gone to reply, so I applied my pressure. I planted one hand between her thighs and slowly threaded upwards.

"Mhm, I am…I, shit."

Shit indeed, my queen.

Between her thighs were warm, as I sucked on her neck, definitely leaving a mark for her to reminisce with. She did the unexpected, she turned.

I half expected her to recognize me, but I prayed she wouldn't. Then I realized she was checking me out. A broad smile cast way across my face, she blushed instantly. Those deep, brown eyes of hers were everything. She was pressed up against me still.

"Like what you see, love?" I don't know how she could be this confident dancing with me like a grown woman, and now she looked like a little school girl, all shy and in her shell.

"May I buy you a drink?" Well then, I wasn't expecting that response. Definitely a first. *She looked nervous though,* as if saying that was an accident.

"I would be lying if I said that a beautiful woman had ever bought me a drink. That's definitely my role." God, I said the corniest shit when I was around her. S*hiiiit, it looked like I offended her.* "Since you're absolutely breath-taking, I'll accept the offer. Just so you know, next time will be on me, princess," She looked happy again. *Thank God.*

I was so captivated by Terriana that I almost missed the sight of the asshat strolling through the dance floor, the sea of bodies parting for him. My face must have changed because she looked at me puzzled, as if sensing my worry. "It seems like I will be finding you in a short while. You and your friend need to leave the club immediately and go straight home," I whispered in her ear. I almost forgot I was surrounded by my department. *Damn, I took my earpiece out.*

She tried to see what I was so worried about, but I held her firmly in place. I couldn't have her seen by him if this went south; that would only cement his grave I wanted to dig. I could see the little sassiness she hid under

40

her sweet exterior peeking out. I officially offended her, *and she was about to let me have it.* "Excuse me?" She was even cuter when she was mad. Her eyes were scrunched tightly. Her nose did a little flare and, Lord, she was a lip-biter, but I couldn't do this now. She needed to go.

"Hey?" I whispered. "Get your friend and get going now, gorgeous. Some very bad people just walked in. I'll come find you," I gave her an 'I dare you to argue look.'

She bit that lip of hers again and pulled away from me. I missed her already. "What if you're the very bad person?" With that said, she walked away from me. A part of me wondered if she recognized me and a part of me wondered if she already realized that she was too good for me. Both analysis scared me. I wanted a chance to show her how hard I would work to be good enough for her *and she wasn't even mine yet.* I wanted to pull her back in my arms and apologize for wanting her to leave, but it was for the best.

As she was out of view, I headed towards our table, discreetly putting my earpiece in. *Sigh.* "Hey, Jason. What am I looking for tonight? Slim, thick, short?" I said loud enough for him to hear. He looked up from the bar, with a girl's tits leaning forward in front of him.

"My man Leo is picking up the girl tonight. You can just go piss off for now." He said nonchalantly, gesturing to Leo sitting nearby. *Dirty prick.*

"Come on. I'm on a roll here. Besides, I'm way better looking. I can get one in record timing." I said with the cockiest smirk I could muster up.

"Fine," he said smoothly.

The plan was going smoothly. He was about to add something else, but I felt a quick tension. Then my partner screamed "Gun, six o'clock" in my ear. A blond doe-eyed girl stepped up into the booth and opened fire.

Bang! Bang! Bang! Bang!

Chapter 5
Terriana

Fuck it!

My brain registered the danger that I needed distance from, but my legs did the opposite. *PTSD at the worst possible time.* Jess slammed into me, jolting me forward. She instinctively held my body up, and she was screaming in my ear, but I couldn't hear her. I couldn't hear anything as a matter of fact. I guess the next thing was inevitable; the bitch-slap that was heard around the world. Yes, that was exactly what Jess did. "Bitch, we have to go. Someone's shooting!" Jess yelled as if I was deaf or something. I didn't get a second to nurse my cheek as I was hauled through a throng of scared high-off-life mob. As the cold air slapped me, I released the breath I didn't realize I was holding.

Then it hit me. How would he find me if I went home? I was almost shot, and here I was praying he would find me so I could thank him. I didn't even know his name. *Shit.*

I sought the faces in the crowd around me. For a shooting that just happened mere minutes ago, there were

43

a lot of police already there. "Terri, what are you doing? Let's go."

"But I don't see him. I didn't get to give him my number," I say with a little wine. *'Thank him with my number,'* I internally smirked.

"Next time. If it's meant to be, you'll see him again, Juliet," she sneered at me. She used the worst time to be a smart ass. *I suppose I picked the worst time to be enamoured.*

The shooting that happened at the club was on the news the next day. The headline read, *"New drug king arrested on four counts of murder and twenty suspected cases including human trafficking."* Just imagine clubbing with a murderer. Makes you want to stay home on a Friday night.

A knock on my office door pulled me out of my haze. I had just finished with my last client for the week, so I had no idea who it would be. "Come in," I said. It couldn't be threatening. Only clients or other office owners had access cards to come up to this floor.

"Hello, Terri. I believe this is for you." Bluebells, my favorite flowers, were being placed on my desk by Cindi, who was also a therapist three doors down from me.

"Thank you. They're beautiful, but I don't understand," I said while bringing the bouquet closer and examining it for a card.

"They were delivered to my office this morning, but by the time I got around to calling my husband to thank him, he was clueless. I realized it had a card attached and noticed it wasn't for me. Sorry." She must have read my still puzzled face, so she continued.

"Bluebells are my favorite too. The doorman knows that, so he obviously assumed these were mine. Am sorry I had them so long." I looked up at her sympathetically and also a little amused. I had never received flowers before, and I had never met another person who loved Bluebells like me.

"Oh, that's okay. No harm no foul and I wasn't expecting flowers. Thank you. Your husband sounds sweet also." I smiled up at her, trying to open the card. A man who sends you flowers, *no wonder you're always happy and glowing.* I got the card opened, and I started doing somersaults in my head.

Hello, Queen. I think that suits you better than princess. You owe me a drink, but I'll treat you to dinner instead. La Bonita. Tonight at 7. Ask for Frankie. —the good guy.

45

How can a girl say no, right? I realized Cindi was now hovering over me. "Thank you for bringing the flowers, Cindi," I gave her that 'you can leave now' look.

"So, are you going to go?" She asked suggestively, truly invested in my business now I suppose.

"Am...I don't know. I don't even know his name," I started to think worst-case scenario now. How did he know where I worked? Or who I was for that matter? Plus, how did he know I was in the club with a 'friend,' not 'friends' and, most importantly, how did he know my favorite flower?

"That's why people date, child, to get to know someone," Cindi said breaking my concentration.

"I suppose you're correct," I said, playing with the note in my hand.

After speaking to Cindi, which mostly consisted of her talking me off a ledge and her gushing about her husband, I gathered my things, closed the office, and made my way next door to Jessica's. Now I would have to give details about that steamy dance floor. *Just kill me now!* I was about to die of embarrassment anyway.

46

Chapter 6
Vinte

Four shots, all in the air, and the room erupted in chaos. I clutched the gun and wrung it out of her grasp easily. But what was the play? I needed to think fast: keep my cover and arrest her and blow the whole operation or play it cool? Everyone was waiting on my signal to close in anyways. "Who the fuck is this bitch?" I yelled and pushed her on the ground towards Jason.

The girl looked up and went crazy. "You fucking bastard. You kidnapped my sister. I know you did. I saw you. You drugged her, and you took her." She was grabbing at him, hitting him on his chest, and screaming in his face while the club cleared out. *I wondered if she was alright.* "She called me today. Said she doesn't know where she is, and that a guard took pity and let her call me." *Bingo*, we can trace that call. It was my lucky day. "Answer me, you sick fuck. Answer me. You beat her, starved her, and you're keeping them in chains."

This whole time, Jason was only blocking her hits and letting her talk. Fuck, he wanted to see what she knew before he killed her. I needed to break this up. I had enough for a bust, search warrant, and prison time charges.

"*Angel face*, you obviously have the wrong guy. We don't know what you're talking about," I said, signally in the cavalry. She completely ignored me and continued attacking him.

"Police! Everybody, hands where I can see them now!" My captain yelled. I immediately raised my hands. Keeping my cover could be beneficial in the future for another case. I got handcuffed, pushed around and a solid fist to the gut from my partner. *I knew that was for coming off script and taking my earpiece out.* When she pushed me outside and led me to the squad car, it was like I felt my girls' presence. I wiggled around in the car seat and spotted her, looking around like she lost something. Her friend looked frantic, like she wanted to jump out of her skin, *but not my girl.* Her friend was saying something, but I couldn't make her lips out. It was going to be a long night, sigh. With the taste of her salty little neck still lingering on the tip of my tongue, I relaxed and got comfortable. *It was about to be a very long night indeed; booking, interrogations, paperwork, shoot me now.*

A long-ass ride to the precinct, getting dragged out of the squad car kicking and playing the tough guy,

48

booking, fingerprinting and, my personal favorite, stripping down butt naked. What can I say, my body was a work of art, toned and sculpted to perfection. As I sat in my cell, getting a little impatient, how long did it take IT to do a simple cell phone track? Roughly four hours later, my partner strolled in. "We got them," she said, all happy with herself, like I haven't been rotting in this cell.

"We better have, if you got me in here rotting unnecessarily for over three freaking hours!" I yelled, well aware that the other jailers were transferred over to county two hours ago.

"Stop being a pussy. We had to go get the other girls he had locked up. We found nine of them, including the crazy girl's sister." She said while closing the cell behind me.

"Where did she even come from? I've been running with them for months and I've never seen her." She seemed genuine, but I wasn't prepared to leave anything to dumb luck.

"Her sister was taken the night you first went undercover with them. You weren't there when it all went down, which is also a plus. They can't tie you with her if this all blows up in our faces." She had this worried look on her face, and with good reason.

49

"I know it was risky going undercover to expose our own. That's why I had to be the one to do it. I moved up rank quickly and am easily overlooked as a rookie. No one knows me. So, stop worrying. I wasn't made." She looked at me like I was crazy, but deep down I knew she knew I was right.

The team drilled asshat Jason for hours before he finally cracked. We had all the evidence needed; all the videos obtained to bury him for life. Plus, best believe we had nine women in witness protection waiting to take the stand and identify him as their kidnapper, pimp and, sometimes, rapist. We had him by the balls, and he knew it. I eventually got tired of the good cop bad cop tactic and left them to handle the rest. After all, I served him up on a silver platter. What could go wrong?

We had the names of the dirty cops, and they were arrested the same time he was being arrested by the FBI. However, God bless them after internal affairs gets through with them. We made the biggest arrest of the decade today, but all I wanted to do was touch her again. Wrap my fingers around her neck and watch her beg me to fuck her. *I had it bad.*

I went home and pulled out a glass from the kitchen, added two ice chips and headed towards my playroom. Pulled a bottle of whisky from under the bar table and poured out a handsome amount. My playroom consisted of all my essential unwinding toys. My Baldwin sits facing the floor to ceiling window, bar to the right of it, a punching bag to the right of the bar and finally a flat screen with the best game console known to man in the other corner. Let off steam on my punching bag, wallow in self-pity at the bar, play my heart out on the piano or block out the world in games. Bulletproof man cave; all I had to do was pick my poison.

Long story short, it didn't work. By the time three in the morning peeped in, I was tired of trying to clear my head of her. I was tired of battling my inner demons on how good I could be for her. It was like trying not to want her had me craving her. So how do I go about having *her*?

I woke the next morning with her on my mind; her face, her smile and the way she held on to me when we danced. I got up and headed for the shower. I was surely making a move on her today, no doubt about it.

After getting ready, I made quick breakfast while lacing up my boots. After loading the dishwasher, I grabbed my gun, badge and keys from off the coffee table and then out the door. I got up a little later than my normal run hour but earlier than my work hour for only one reason. There was a flower shop around the corner from my condo, and if I got there fast enough, I could be first in line. Everyone knew early birds catch the most worms, in my case, I could get the nicer flowers and not what everyone had left behind. I parked out front so I could be in and out, but then it hit me. I had no romantic bone in my body, and I didn't know what kind of flowers she liked. I may have done research on her, but only textbook stuff, public records, not stalk your trash.

My whole spirit deflated in one thought. I walked in no less and looked around a little. There were so many choices. Thank God for labels or I wouldn't know a Lily from a Dandelion. Then I saw them, blue like the dress she wore the first time I saw her and pretty as can be. *Does she even like flowers though?* Well, here goes nothing I guess. I got two bunches and wrote a note:

(First attempt)

Hello Princess, I am so sorry for not staying around after everything got so crazy. Have dinner with me…

Hell no. Too cheesy.

(Second attempt)

Hello Love, I really enjoyed last night. Am sorry I had to send you away so abruptly. Let's get lunch together…

Fucking hell. I sound like a punk.

(Third attempt)

52

Hello Queen, I think that suits you better than princess. You owe me a drink, but I'll treat you to dinner instead. La Bonita, tonight at 7. Ask for Frankie. —the good guy.

Yes, that will do.

Now on to phase two. A couple restaurant owners owed me a favor or two, *am cashing in today.* It was always a beautiful thing to save a life, but when those lives offered you free meal whenever you want, it made it so much more fun to interact with people. So, I made the reservations from my Bluetooth car speaker while turning into the precinct. Looking at my watch I saw that it was seven fifty. She should be making her way into her office, and if the delivery guy makes good on the extra twenty dollars I tipped him, the flowers should already be on her desk.

"Eww, is that how you look when you smile," I heard the sound of my annoying partner breaking through my good mojo. I ignored her and headed to our office. I knew she was going to follow me and stare me down from her desk, but I was in a good mood. "I don't think I've ever seen you smile before, now that I think about it. Sammie, have you ever seen this dick smile before?"

I shook my head. She was drawing attention to me, *seriously.* I glared at her. "Never. Must have gotten some last night. After all, he did hightail it out of here after his big bust and all."

"You both know am sitting right here, and I can hear you?" I said, drawing my words for emphasis.

"So," they both said simultaneously as if to annoy me.

I ignored them for the most part, then my partner, Jay, short for Naejay, asked the most dumbfounded question, "Are you serious about this girl?"

I really didn't know how to answer. Jay had seen the revolving door of women I had entertained, *so to speak*. After all, I didn't date, but I guess she felt the need to ask after I skipped protocol and finally danced with her. Jay had been my angel and devil's advocate every time I got near to her. But last night, when she released me from lock up, it was like she knew. She didn't even bitch when I said I was going home.

"I asked her out on a date," I said, looking up for her reaction.

"How will you play this? Tell her you're a cop or hide it?" I knew she would ask that. It was my first challenge when I first realized I liked her.

"Hide it, well, downplay it if it comes up. I don't want to spook her," I said with a sigh.

"Mhmm, you're a detective. We live by being anonymous. If she isn't like all the rest, then that same statement can be dangerous. So I ask again, Vin, are you serious about this girl?" She paused, then added, "You can't build a relationship on a lie, if that's what you want."

I know exactly what she meant. If she didn't know in the beginning, she might leave me for lying or she might get hurt if any of my covers got blown. "Think we're getting ahead of ourselves. I don't even know if she will show up later or if she's interested. We're talking like she's mine already." *Sigh*.

"Isn't she?" Jay added with a knowing smirk. "Besides, with the way she was leaning into you and moaning, she definitely coming tonight, pun intended, ha!"

"Shit! You heard all of that!" I said in a mini panic.

"Hell, yes. I specially turn it up when it got super cheesy *'Are you always this stunning even in the dark, gorgeous?'* I don't think I've ever laughed that hard, Mr. Smooth." I was beat red from embarrassment, not for me but, *for her*. "Don't worry, Romeo. I was the only one listening. Only wanted to make sure you were good."

After I went home to freshen up and change for dinner, I made my way to the restaurant. I just might die if she stood me up tonight. She had my balls in her hand and she didn't even know it yet. We had the most intimate table in the room, a small, secluded area near the back, with a floor-to-ceiling window overlooking the ocean; perfect view.

It was six fifty-five and I was getting really anxious. I started surveying the room a little. There was a small commotion but I couldn't see what it was. *Keep it together. You've been out before, and you've screwed enough women without even looking at them, so man up.* I heard light taps approaching my section of the restaurant. In that moment, I knew exactly what the commotion was about. *Merciful Father, send help.*

Chapter 7
Terriana

"You look absolutely stunning," he said, putting me at ease. I was so tongue tide, lost in his manly musk of cologne and spices.

"Thank you. You look really good too," I was barely audible. I was holding in the urge to jump him right then and there. He had a steel-like stare, as if he only had eyes for me. I felt partly embarrassed for the host being stuck looking between us.

"Thanks, Frankie. You can send someone over in a bit, please." I bet she felt relieved being excused.

"No problem, Vin. You two enjoy now. Let me know if you need anything," she replied with a smile.

So his name is Vin! One question down.

"Thank you for coming. Take a seat." He not only stood for my arrival, but he pulled out a chair for me. *I guess chivalry isn't dead.*

"Thank you. This view is amazing isn't it?" I sat and painfully tore my eyes off his handsome physique and the way his clothes looked tailor-made and hot.

57

"Yes, it is," he replied. Not only was he ignoring the view I was referring to, but his eyes were locked on me and never wavered; so captivating. I didn't need a mirror to tell me I was crimson red in the face. My lady parts even tingled making me cross my legs to bury the building pressure.

"How did you know where I worked?" I needed the distraction, and this question was red hot on my list.

"The security guard at the club knows your friend." I got the feeling there was more to it, but the night was still young.

"And the Bluebells?" his face showed worry, like it did at the club.

"I don't understand. *God*, you didn't like them? I'm sorry…" he was worried.

"No, no, I loved them actually. They're my favorite. How did you know?" I loved bluebells. Where I was from, they were the only flowers that bloomed near my house.

"I didn't," he replied simply. I looked down. His facial expression seemed sincere, but I didn't want him to catch me blushing again.

"When I first laid eyes on you, it was as if I couldn't breathe all my life and finally found a pocket of air. Then when I held you on the dance floor, *God,* I had to know you."

Damn. I thought it was my subconscious, *but he felt it too.* "Well, that makes two of us," I said with a little giggle. I couldn't help it. *I liked him.* "My name is Terriana Watson. It's a pleasure to formally meet you," I bit my lip and stuck my hand out for him.

"Vinte Sanchez. A pleasure to finally meet you." He took my hand, and that feeling of a safe haven overcame my body. *What was he doing to me?*

"It's been less than twenty-four hours since our first dance, *Vinte,*" I tested his name. *It was different.* "You're staring." He was more like gawking, but I liked it. There was something primal about it.

"So sorry to interrupt. Is the lovely couple ready to order dinner?" asked the waitress, startling me out of my trance. *When did she get here?*

"We're not dating," I said, way too quickly, I might admit.

I caught a little smirk from him. He welcomed my challenge, like he was saying, '*Let's play.*'

"Not yet," he added with a smile.

Shit, he caught me blushing again.

"I'm sorry, I only assumed," the waitress replied staring down at the table. My eyes wandered to the waitress. She looked a little nervous, yet a little knowing, as if she knew something we didn't. I knew what I wanted to order, but I never checked the menu if they had it. I looked at the table for the menu and found something else entirely different. He was still holding my hand, stroking it oh so delicately. I almost couldn't feel it. Realization then dawned on me. I looked up and found Vinte looking at me with the same stupefied look I knew I was wearing. I really didn't want to pull away. His touch was intoxicating. I wondered how it would feel if his finger got a chance to explore more than just my hand. "May we have a couple more minutes to ponder the menu, please?" The waitress nodded in his direction, then turned and walked away.

"How was your day?" He asked.

I no longer cared for small talk. My body liked him. There was no doubt about that, but I had been too lonely to have someone waltz in and disturb my peace for the wrong reasons. "It was a good day. How'd you know that there was going to be trouble?" I didn't need to go further. The way his grip tightened and his throat bobbed, I could tell he was caught by surprise. Being a psychologist, I learned how to tell tails. I saw that he had restraint, but I was better.

60

"A part of my job is to know things. I know that wasn't the answer you were hoping for, but it's all am able to give. Am sorry." Also another sincere answer, but the truth could be hidden with a really good lie. I stopped grilling him after that. One question led to another, and we talked the night away about everything and nothing at the same time.

Chapter 8
Vinte

*D*amnnn! She looked like a goddess. She had on these fuck-me shoes again. An army green dress with a high slit to the side, and her breast were beautifully displayed. Her hair looked nice and bouncy and she just looked amazing. *like a work of art, wow!*

As she walked up to me with the confidence draining off her face and replaced with a very innocent shyness, I stood up for her. *Not like that.* I stretched out my hand for her and just couldn't wait any longer, "You look absolutely stunning."

I could visibly see her shoulders relaxed. "Thank you. You look really good too," She whispered out to me.

I was about to reply when I realised Frankie was still standing there with us. "Thanks, Frankie. You can send someone over in a bit, please."

Frankie was the store manager and a good friend of mine now. "No problem, Vin. You two enjoy now. Let me know if you need anything."

I replied with a smile. I had never brought a woman there before. I had never dated, so I never had a need to, *before now anyways.*

"Thank you for coming. Take a seat," I said while pulling her chair out for her.

"Thank you. This view is amazing, isn't it?"

"Yes, it is," I replied while looking dead in her eyes.

She blushed and batted her lashes, hook, line and sinker. "How did you know where I worked?" I was prepared for this question, *just not yet.*

"The security guard at the club knows your friend." I really didn't want to lie to her, so I left it right there at the truth.

"And the Bluebells?" Oh, she was going in, no nonsense.

"I don't understand, *God*, you didn't like them? I'm sorry…" I was screwed.

"No, no. I loved them actually. They're my favourite. How did you know?"

"I didn't." I replied simply. She bowed her head, hiding her eyes from me, *cute*. "When I first laid eyes on you, it was as if I couldn't breathe all my life and finally found a pocket of air. Then when I held you on the dance

64

floor, *God,* I had to know you." *Damn, I really didn't mean to say that much.*

"Well, that makes two of us." She said with a little giggle. "My name is Terriana Watson. It's a pleasure to formally meet you." She bit her lip and stuck her hand over the table.

"Vinte Sanchez. A pleasure to finally meet you." Am cheesing on the inside, trying to keep myself as calm as possible.

"It's been less than twenty-four hours, *Vinte.*" The way she tests my name on her lips, pure seduction. "You're staring."

And you're gorgeous.

"So sorry to interrupt. Is the lovely couple ready to order dinner?" Said the waitress way too close. *How did she sneak up on me? When did she even get over here?*

"We're not dating."

Okay, Terriana. I'll play.

"Not yet," I added with a smile to Terriana. Oh, I loved it when she blushed.

"I'm sorry. I only assumed," the waitress replied, staring down at something on the table. My eyes wandered in the direction she stared at, and a sense of relief consumed me. I had been holding her hand and stroking the back with my thumb this whole time and didn't even realise it. The best part, she was letting me. Then she looked down at our hand, and I watched as realization dawned on her too. Will she pull away? She just looked up at me from under her long lashes instead.

"May we have a couple more minutes to ponder the menu, please?" I watched as the waitress nodded politely at me, then turned to walk away.

"How was your day?"

That was how we started the evening, light conversation with some really good food. Plus, I discovered she actually ate food, not pick at it like girls I had tried taking out, *and boy won't I start cooking up a storm again.*

She had the right amount of plump in all the right places, with a tiny waist that I was dying to put my hands around again. "You're eye-fucking me," she said with a little sass and a little flirtatiousness that I had to decipher between in the last hour we talked for.

"Language, miss." She squirmed a little. With a body like hers, how could I resist eye-fucking her? One thing for sure though, if she rolled her eyes, crisscrossed her legs, or bit her lip again, I was taking her on this table.

"I was admiring you," I said with a small chuckle.

66

"Stripping me naked with your eyes was more like it," she said with her martini straw lightly tapping her tongue.

"Would you prefer my hands?" I asked with a smirk. I visibly saw her swallow, hard, her thighs were pressed together, and she was flushed.

Before I could add something, she pushed off the table. "Excuse me, I have to use the little lady's room."

Oh, she was good, sexy as hell, smart, she gave to charity, she was an orphan and loved dogs but didn't own one. I think I had uprooted more information on her in an hour than on my partner who I was with every day. As she walked away with an extra swing in her hips, I realized that she either had on a thong or going commando. Her dress hugged her hips way too smoothly, and her fuck-me-heels were doing a number on my dick. *Lord, please make her hurry back and not slip out on me.*

When I got her here, I expected to lose interest in her like I did with all the others before her. Then I realized like ten minutes in that I was comparing her to women I never dated but took out once, fucked and never spoke to again, unless it was for seconds. That wasn't what I wanted for her. I felt a strong urge to protect and care for her. She appealed to all my senses. *She was like a craving, addictive.*

Three minutes had passed along with my patience. I pushed back on the chair, and before I got up to find her, I saw her golden legs strutting back to me. *Racy as hell.* She batted her eyes and sat her purse down on the table. I stood and she sat. Looking up at me from behind her long lashes had me wondering if she would look this good on her knees, with her lips wrapped around my cock, looking up at me like she was now. *I think I was tired of wondering.*

"I never really go out, you know." She appeared to be fighting an internal battle, as if she was unsure about something.

"Likewise, but I really enjoyed your company tonight. Would you like to go for a drive, extend the night a bit?" I needed more time with her; *don't judge me.*

"Okay, I like driving so this should be fun."

I paid the bill and laced my hand at the small of her back leading her outside towards the valet. My hand had been itching to touch her all night. I missed her touch and scent; she smelt good.

The valet parked my car, BMW Z4. I opened her door and she slid in. I went around and entered the car to see her smiling from ear to ear. "This car has an eight-speed automatic transmission with sport mode as well as

68

manual mode. Paddle shifters mounted to the steering wheel are also standard," she said so sexily.

Sex on wheels: *Is she trying to make us crash? She speaks cars, damn, I think I got a hard on.*

"You speak cars?" I replied.

"I grew up in a mechanic shop, so I can fix them too," she said giddily. I smiled. This little tit-for-tat flirting and light conversation had me cheesing.

"Is that so? What else should I know about you, love?" Shit, I look at her in the mirror, trying to see if that slip of endearment registered with her.

"I'm pretty handy is all. A little of a do-it-myselfer." That was about to change.

"I find that a do it 'yourselfer' comes from not having someone to help. Day or night, am your guy," I said as cocky as possible.

"You have all the right comebacks, don't you? Probably go on dates often," she replied, watching me from her eye corner.

So now she was silently asking if I was playing her. "I won't lie and say I've never met a girl and pursued her until I've bed her, but I've also never wanted to date anyone as much as I want to take you out again, and again, and again."

She seemed nervous playing with her purse, looking everywhere except at me. "You really have a comeback for it all," she giggled.

"I am a man of my word. I will always tell you the truth, and right now, you're teasing me." I look in the mirror for her reaction, but I only get her side profile.

"How am I teasing you?" she replied without turning to look at me, and crossed her legs, showing a little more skin than before.

"You know exactly what you're doing," I replied, touching on the gas a little harder.

We had been driving around and, subconsciously, I ended up at my condo, parked on the sidewalk. "I've been dying to kiss you all night." The words were out before I could hold them back.

"So do it," she said, looking up at me for the first time in half an hour. I unbuckled my seat belt, then hers, and leaned into her, over the console. I gazed straight in her eyes, giving her a final chance to back out before I rocked her world. I crashed my lips on hers as if she was water and I was on fire. She moaned, and that gave me the opening I needed to deepen the kiss. I tasted her lips and massaged her tongue with my own. My fingers found their way into her hair to hold her in place. When I finally

70

pulled away, we were panting and her lips were a little swollen. I took pride knowing it was because of me.

As I watched her breathing even and her finally opening those beautiful eyes of hers, I immediately wanted more. I planted small kisses on her, from her ear to the corner of her lips, then crashed down on her lips again, this time with a desire I didn't see coming. Tender, passionate and lustful could describe the way I was attacking her mouth. When I pulled away, her lips were now inflated and cherry pink.

"Would you like to come up to my condo… to talk some more, I mean?"

Oh, fuck me!

Here I was trying to be a gentleman, and look what I asked her.

"I don't think that's a good idea. I'm trying really hard not to be easy. I don't think I'll have any will power being alone with you."

I smiled at her honesty, "Here I am trying to be a gentleman myself. It's like I was on autopilot driving you to my home. Sorry about that, Terri. I know how it looks," I tested her name aloud for the first time.

She pursed her lips and got out of the car so fast I panicked. I got out and went around to her. She had her back pressed up on the car door and head falling down hiding her face from me. I went and stood boldly in front of her. I used my fingertips to push back her hair, then tipped her head up to face me. "What's going on in that pretty head of yours?" I was dying to know. I felt as if I had upset her or scared her, and that was the last thing I wanted.

She stared at me, like she was trying to read my soul. "I've never done this before, but I want to." She gave me a small smile and pushed off the car, crashing her lips on mine. I licked, I sucked, and I nibbled on her lips while my hands roamed as much of her body as possible while pinning her back on the car. One of her legs started to climb up my side, and I took it as an invitation to lift her up. With my hands on her ass, she wrapped her legs around me beautifully. I could spank her, *in fact.*

SWAT!

"Mmmhm," she moaned into my mouth, and I spun and made my way to my front door with that extra courage. I fumbled to open the door and slammed it shut behind us. There was something about her delicate hands on me that had such an innocent feel to it. I pushed up her dress to reveal her plump ass. She pulled my ear in her mouth while I stared at her ass in one of my hall mirrors. Black lacy thong, *bite me.* "Fuck," I whispered

72

when I felt her tongue in my ear. I opened my room door and stepped in. I sat her down on her feet and stared at her, letting my eyes adjust to the darkness.

"Did I do something wrong?" she whispered with a raspy voice, probably from all that kissing.

I smiled at my handy work, "God, no." I pulled her by the arm while walking backwards towards my bed. When I got to the bed, I sat at the edge, still raking my eyes over her, pure perfection, even with her dress bunched above her hips and her hair a little messier. *All mine.* "Strip for me." I think that sounded a little masochistic, but she obliged. She pulled her dress down and then unbuttoned it, from her glorious breast all the way down to her upper thighs where it ended. She relaxed her shoulders, and looked dead in my eyes as the dress fell to the ground and pooled around her heals. *Am in trouble?*

"More?" she whispered, barely audible.

"I'll do the rest." I shrugged out of my shirt, not bothering to unbutton it. I just pulled and sent the buttons flying. She shivered and bit her lip, panting, which made the swell of her breast more visible. I stepped out of my slacks and stood in front of her butt-naked. Unlike her thong, I went commando. She took me in from head to head, and her reaction was perfect, timid and unsure of herself. "Do you want us to stop? I wouldn't object if you did?" I really didn't want to pressure her. After all, this was our first date. I stretched and turned the side lights on dim. When I looked back, she was already at me. She took my lips with a hunger I really didn't anticipate with how reserved she was on our date. I matched her pressure with my lips as she climbed up on me, legs at both sides straddling my thighs. I took the opportunity to make quick work of her bra. I had one hand in her hair and the other squeezing her ass cheek. The sweet sound of her moans and purrs of pleasure started to fill the room, edging me on as well.

I pulled away from her lips and latched on to her right nipple, running the hand that was in her hair down the center of her back oh so gently. I felt her back arching more into me, with her firm butt cheek sitting nicely in my palm, being palmed. "Vinte," she barely mouthed out in my ear. That was all it took. I flipped her onto the bed on her back, and made sure she was comfortable under me, with her legs still spread like a kite at either side.

"Are you sure? Do you want to stop?"

She shook her head no, but I needed to hear it, as if she heard my plea. "No, please don't stop. Just be gentle." As if a bell rang in my ear, her earlier words came flooded back, 'I've never done this before.'

74

Wait, "Are you a…?" I couldn't say the words. I was too caught off guard.

"Um, no, um, well, I don't have much practice is all." I looked at her long and hard for an inkling of a doubt; there was none.

"Are you sure?" I asked for the final time.

"Yes, am sure."

That was all I needed. I leaned in on her and our lips connected like two pieces of a jigsaw and moved in harmony. I explored every inch of her mouth, kneading her breast with one hand while the other caressed the length of her body. I felt her panties and gripped it firmly and in one quick motion ripped them off. She gasped into my mouth, and I gladly swallowed. I threw her undies somewhere on the floor and began leaving tiny wet kisses on her neck, while my hand ran along her curved outline from her breast slowing down to her mid-thigh. Then I began threading my fingers back up her inner thigh. She was still, for the most part, panting, trying to steady herself I bet. I was about to worship her body and she had no idea. I stopped my hand movement just shy of her bud. I don't know how inexperienced she was, but I knew one thing: I might not have been her first but am about to be her fucking last, so help me God.

I pushed up off her. She was spread open like a starfish, simply immaculate. Her hair a little disheveled, eyes watching my every movement, lips swollen, full perky breast, flat stomach, and the prettiest cunt I had ever seen. Her legs were short, but sexy as hell. As I knelt in between her thighs, admiring her, I recognized the spark of hunger in her eyes as she licked her lips. She was hot and frustrated as much as I was.

I hovered over her and kissed her square on her lips and made my way south of the border. When I got to her navel, I stopped and clapped my hands. Light music trickled in from the surround sound. I could hear her pant and moan as clear as day regardless, plus it seemed to do the trick of relaxing her. I resumed my attacks on her body, parting her lips with my tongue, bracing open her legs with my hands. "I have the best view now," I said, then licked her in one smooth motion from the opening to her clitoris, pulling it into my mouth and then releasing with a pop. I felt her body arch off the bed as she exhaled and strained out a moan. I needed her dripping harder than a faucet.

I pushed my hands under her ass for support to hold her steady and pushed my face into her thighs, sucking and licking between her folds. I pushed my tongue as far as I could. She was so tight I could feel the pressure building in her cries of pleasure, sweet music to my ears.

76

She tightened her legs around my head like a vice. I pulled out a hand from her ass and wet my finger playing with her folds and slowly entered her. "Fuck, you are tight." Like I knew it, but damn, seeing was believing right.

I latched on to her clit while slowly moving in and out of her. She was panting like crazy at this point. "Vin, I'm…." She threw her head back unable to finish her sentence.

"I know, baby. Just a little more." *God, she looked amazing*, sweaty, flushed, and writhing from my touch. Like the devil I was, I slid another finger in. I let her adjust while licking on her clit from left to right while pumping my fingers into her. I could feel her pulling on the sheets in agony. "Vintee," she cried out.

"Come." She did just that. It was like she was rendered speechless, no sound. I slowly pulled my fingers out and listened to her gasping for air now tugging on my hair.

I slowly kissed my way up her body, giving her time to come down from her high. She was breathtaking, responsive as hell, and oh so wet for me. I kissed slowly, passionately. I didn't want her to think this was a one-night stand. This was a far cry from that, *incomparable.* I opened the side table and pulled out a condom. I made quick work of it as I positioned at her opening, waiting for her. "Are you okay?" I breathed out. I was panting and nervous for some reason. I had done this so many times, but I had never really done it in this position now that I thought about it. It was more personal like this, I suppose. If I pushed even an inch, I could be inside her, but it was her call.

"I'm more than okay. Go on." She didn't even give me a second to process. She impounded on my lips, and I gripped her left ass, bracing it open, while painfully inching into her. Her walls were squeezing the life out of me beautifully. Her breathing was short and loud. *I smiled into the kiss.* I wasn't going to last long. Her nails dug into me, one in my side and the other my shoulder. "Fuck!" she screamed.

"Am I hurting you?" I eased out and back in a couple of times, never going too far. "Terriana?" I couldn't hold back any fucking longer. Before she could answer, I pulled out and pushed all the way in to the hilt and steadied myself holding her. She cried out and dug into me more. *Jack move, I know,* but I had to rip the band-aid off somehow.

As I felt her body relax a little, I started rocking into her. Her hands began roaming around my back, sending more tension to my dick. I was going to burst faster than I thought. I hiked her left leg up over my hip with her heels digging into my calves. I began grinding into her, making sure to rub on her clit. Her moans were melodic, our breathlessness in sync, and I felt her getting tighter, if possible, signaling that she was close. With my left thigh keeping her open and her right leg tightly hooked around me, I pushed one hand into her hair, one kneading her breast, and latched my lips on her neck. "Vin!" One hard suck on her neck and I was balls-deep inside, her coating my cock and soaking my bed. Three more thrust had me collapsing on top of her, not too much to crush her, just enough to cuddle, still inside her. She was breathless.

I got up and discarded the condom and went straight back into the bed, pulled the covers over us and pulled her to my side. "That was, um, it was, God. Help me out here."

She was out of breath and cute. "Amazing, but go to sleep. You need some rest. We can talk in the morning." I could feel her smiling into my neck as we dosed off. Let's just say we got an hour sleep and made a couple more breathless moments, until we ended up finishing the hot water from the shower. When we refueled and actually went to bed, it was 5:30 am.

Chapter 9
Terriana

I cannot believe I just fucked him. *Shit.shit.shit.* I swore I wouldn't, but no self-control struck again. Seriously, Terri, you had a perfectly good pro-con list, for God's sake. *He.was.not.the.one.* You gave yourself such a good pep talk in that bathroom. Firstly, no going home with him. Yes, he was hot as hell, sexy, a smart businessman, who served our country, but for peace's sake, *date number one.*

Here I was, laying in the most comfortable bed known to man, completely wrapped in this man's arms, feeling so safe I could kill someone for interrupting and having no clue how to walk-of-shame my ass out. *Completely embarrassing, I know.* There was no way a guy like him could want me, despite the four mind-blowing times he made love to me and how he worshipped my body all night long. If feeling this drawn to someone was legal, it would have its own warning label. I had it bad, and I needed to leave before he woke up, and I had to endure the 'it isn't you, it's me' monologue.

81

I didn't know this man, but God knows it would break me if he did it. I didn't know why I surrendered myself to him like that last night. I had never done that before, ever. My first, who will never be mentioned, never did half of what he did to my body. I had aches in places I didn't know aches could be in, and regardless of the soreness, I was still pinned under him and wouldn't have it any other way.

I slowly pulled my arm out and pulled the sheet down so I only had one arm and leg free. He covered the rest of me. I slowly tried to pull out from under him without him waking up. "Where are you going?"

Crap! Too late.

"I, um, was am..." He pulled me in closer before I could get my words out. His breath fanning the side of my face had me hot and bothered. I bit my lip, remembering last night's dinner. He looked so good sitting at the table, almost nervous. His entire face lit up when he saw me. His eyes roamed every inch of my body, setting each spot on fire. When I was close enough, he reached out for my hand.

"Good morning, Terri." I heard the faint words being whispered in my ear, followed by sweet, sweet kisses being left on my neck.

"Good morning," I replied, a little more hoarse than desired. I must have fallen asleep again. For a once street kid, I should know better than to fall asleep in unknown territories.

"Are you always this gorgeous in the morning?"

I pealed my eyes open to look up into the most beautiful hazel eyes I had ever seen. I was a little speechless, and it was so embarrassing. "Hi," I blushed.

"Hi," he replied, flashing me those eye-catching pearly whites.

"Stoppp," I whined, pushing my face into his neck.

"Stop what?" he jeered, completely knowing what he was doing.

"Flirting, your hand rubbing my ass, and that!" I whisper yelled when I felt his dick pushing against my inner thigh.

"I vaguely recalled saying that after round two, then I specifically recalled someone feeling brave and wrapping her tiny little hands around my dick, followed by her li..."

"Stoppp. I get it!" I shouted out of mortification, half laughing at my insatiable behaviour. Then I heard the

83

sweetest thing, he laughed, full belly laugh. I pulled away to look and got lost in how cute he looked, then I spotted a dimple. *Aren't I in trouble!*

"Was that the truth, last night?" We already had sex, so he could drop the act now, not sure I was prepared for it, given I was completely wrapped in his arms.

"Yes. I won't ever lie to you." His transition from full on laughter to this sated look was staggering, more so, he knew exactly what I was talking about, no questions asked.

The door pushed open knocking into my heels that was thrown away sometime last night. *Oh yes*, after he first told me to go to bed, he wrapped his body around me and felt it, then took them off.

"Oh, I'm so sorry. I didn't realise you had company," a lady in her mid-thirties, maybe, entered and covered her eyes.

"That's okay, Kim. You would have met eventually." He said that so matter of fact while planting kisses on my exposed shoulder. *God, I wanted him.* "Terriana, meet my housekeeper, Kimberlee. Kim, meet my girlfriend, Terriana."

"What." Both Kimberlee and I replied in unison, with my hands on his chest keeping him from continuing

84

his assault on my back, and now Kimberlee facing us brazenly.

"What" he replied clueless.

"Could we get a moment please, Kim. I need to talk with this little one," he said, tapping me on the nose.

I was in a terrified state. No one had ever called me the 'g' word other than Jessica. *Shit, Jessica!* She must be worried out of her mind. I pushed him off me and sat up, holding the covers to my naked chest. "I need to call my friend before she sends out a search party." Here I was panicking, scanning the room for my bag with my phone and there he was calmer than a cucumber. He then startled me by pushing my hair behind my ear.

"I already spoke to her; your phone was ringing like crazy and I didn't want to wake you. I knew you were tired, so I answered. I hope you don't mind." He said, stroking my cheek.

"Um, what did she say?" I knew what she would say, I just wanted to hear him say it.

"Well, after she finished some choice words before I could say hello, she asked if you were okay. When I told her it was me on the phone, she freaked out again thinking I kidnapped you. Then she told me that if you

85

don't call her before midday, she would report you missing." Yes, that sounded like Jess.

"Here's your phone," he said, handing me my purse.

"Thank you." He sat and waited for me to text her: I was okay. Then the door knocked. He told Kim to enter, and she did with a tray of the most heavenly scents imaginable: bacon, tea, omelettes, fruits, pastries, pancakes, and sweet juicy plantains. After she sat the tray down beside us on the bed, I watched her leave the room with a huge grin on her face, *weirdo*. I still had the sheet pressed to my chest and the rest pooled around my lower back and hiding my legs.

"Let's talk now, while we eat," he said between chews on a strawberry. Oh, he was really good at seduction. The way he bit into the fruit with his lips wrapped around it like they did my, *take your mind out of the gutter*. I began eating with him. After everything we did last night, the food we had early that morning did nothing to quell the hunger. I wasn't sure if I was hungrier for the food or him right now the way he ate. He made everything look sexy.

"This wasn't a one-night stand for me. I wasn't playing you, am not playing you," he said, putting down a piece of bacon. His eyes held a pleading aura.

"I played a role in last night too. I gave in after all," and it was the best release of control in my life.

86

"Yes, but we were drinking, and you had made it clear that you didn't feel comfortable knowing half a story." Was he regretting what happened?

"Do you regret what we did?" I was scared to hear his response and I hated the crack in my voice.

"Hell, no. Last night was the best night of my life."

Mmhm! Is that true?

"Best night or best fuck?" I couldn't help myself.

"Language, little lady."

I bit my lip; the way he said that, so bossy yet endearing. "I said worse last night." I really did. I covered my face; it was redder than the strawberries.

"Yes, you did, but that's different. You're too gorgeous to be cursing so ugly."

Oh, he was really good.

"Last night was the first time I really took a woman out with the intention of not having sex with her." He was lost in thought at this point, almost bearing his soul. "I really tried restraining myself but when you laughed at dinner, I couldn't take not touching you anymore." At this point he had me in the palm of his hands like putty. "I do my job to help people, to defend those who can't defend themselves, and yes, it's a dangerous job that requires me to stand alone most of the time, but am

87

trying to stand by you." No one had ever bared their soul to me like this before. I was in awe. I leaned in and gave him a chaste kiss, showing him what words failed to relay.

"You make me feel safe and wanted. In my book, that's all that matters. Just promise not to hurt me?" No one is perfect and I had known this man a little over twelve hours, not even a full day, so forgive my naive behaviour. "You don't drink coffee?" I asked him, trying to lighten the mood.

"No. I find it's too bitter. Besides, tea comes in so many different flavors. You?"

I smiled and tipped my tea cup to him. "Same," I said, smiling into my mug.

After filling our pallets, he set the tray on the side table. I felt a little self-conscious at this point. I got off the bed with the sheet sprawled around me to cover up as best as possible. "I've seen and kissed every inch of your body," I heard him say, while boring a hole in my back. His words ignited my skin. It was like I could feel every word as a touch. So, I released the sheet.

I heard a small gasp followed by light footsteps creeping up behind me. He pulled my hair back. I felt his breath on my shoulder, then a kiss. His hands wrapped around

88

my waist. He began kissing my neck, *hard,* while one of his hands travelled down. We stood in the middle of his room, floor-to-ceiling windows like mine. I was butt-naked, his chest to my back, his thick, long erection pressed heavily on my lower back covered by his boxers. I felt my legs getting moist from his mild psychological assault on my body. I was so exposed, and then he entered with a finger. It was the most exhilarating feeling I had ever felt. I felt so alive in his arms. With his left hand on my stomach keeping me steady and his right hand wreaking havoc, I wanted to scream.

His heartbeat was racing. With his chain pendant pressed up against my back, I had one hand in his hair pushing him harder on my neck, standing on my toes. My other hand covered his right, pushing him deeper inside me. "Vin!" I screamed out, out of breath and struggling not to come.

"Yes, baby."

Oh, God. What is this stranger doing to me? His hand that held me steady creeped up higher, and with one squeeze to my nipple, *I.came.hard.* "Fuckkkk!" I went limb in his arms but had no time to even breathe. He pushed me on the bed, feet flat on the ground while I was face down. I laid my hands to the side of my head. I heard the crinkling of foil followed by his feet pushing mine wide open. Spread like a sandwich, I looked over my shoulder and saw him looking, no admiring. He leaned down and gave me a sweet chaste kiss on my ass, right cheek then left cheek.

By the time my eyes fluttered closed, I felt a jolt of pain that never felt any better, thick and stiff and mine, *hopefully*. In one fluid stroke, he sank right into me. I gripped the sheets so tight it hurt, and bit down on my lip. This was pleasure because I knew rape.

"Fuckk! How can you feel tighter than last night!" He whisper yelled. He was in sweet pain. His cock was hard and heavy inside me. I felt completely filled. He landed kiss after kiss on my back. I was so lost in him, one hand playing my clit like a piano and the other gripping my hip for dear life. Then he began pumping into me. I arched my ass up more. He moved his hand from my hip to my lower back. I could feel the spine-shattering orgasm building.

"Don't come yet, love."

The fuck was I supposed to do. "I can't hold it," I cried out. I thought he was fucking me last night, but I was so wrong, he was holding back.

KNOCK, KNOCK!

"The fuck," I whispered.

Smack, his hand connected my ass so hard I leaped a little as if the bed wasn't barring me from moving an inch. "Language."

Is he serious right now?

KNOCK, KNOCK, KNOCK!

"Not now, Kim!" He yelled, then he pulled out of me so fast I whimpered. He pulled me off the bed and turned me around. He cupped my butt cheeks and lifted me up. I instinctively wrapped my legs around his waist. I found his lips with a vengeance, our tongues tangled and untangled repeatedly. Then I felt my back pressed against something cold. I pulled away a bit frightened from the feel and from his lips, my fingers matted in his inch-long hair. I was pressed on the window by this time. I felt his cock throbbing at my entrance, begging to be covered. I could feel how drenched I was. I reached down between us and gripped him; he lowered me down on him. "You're insatiable," he breathed in my ear.

I couldn't speak. He felt so good like this, with his muscles flexed, his dick pulsing inside me, sweet inch-by-inch glory of a tool. His heart was racing and we were both panting like crazy. His hand left my ass and wrapped around my throat. I looked him dead in the eye, "Fuck me." I whispered.

"Yes, maam." By the time I came, I saw stars. The monstrous grunt he released when he came was music to my soul.

We showered, we slept, we ate. I called Jess, he gave me a tour, we talked, and then he took me home. Twelve hours turned into twenty-four with him. 6:30p.m Sunday evening caught me at home watching him drive away. *What was that? The most beautiful mistake I had ever made? The best night of my life?* It felt like I was sleeping all my life until I met him. I had never craved anything before, not love, not power, not companionship, nothing, but I wanted him so bad, even with the secrets he owed me, and that scared the hell out of me.

He told me about growing up and how he always felt unloved by his parents, how he could never please them, but how he still loved his mom. I told him about Jess, how she was my sister that I never knew I needed. I couldn't tell him how I met her, but talking with him felt natural. It was like I found myself in him. We talked like we knew each other for years.

As I sat on the floor of my shower washing my hair, I felt a pang of guilt for being home and not wherever he was, but I had a life too. Besides, he was right, we have all the time in the world to run away together and burn out or we could take baby steps and really get to know each other. Shit, I didn't get his number, nor did I pick up my car from that restaurant. *Stupid.*

The phone rang twice before she picked up. "Hey you, am home." It sounded like she was shuffling papers around.

"Okay, am coming over in an hour," she replied as if on autopilot.

"Um, could you pick Merci up for me, please? I left her at the restaurant last night by accident?"

The line was silent, as if she was looking at it, very possible, might I add. "So, you're telling me you left your car at the restaurant, which is a half hour drive in the opposite direction of your house, on top of everything else you did? Are you on crack?"

I deserved that. "Thanks. I'll see you in two hours. Bye." I hung up before she could respond. I knew I wasn't getting out of telling her the details, but I could stall the inevitable.

When she arrived, I had dinner ready and was sitting around my kitchen island with a glass of red wine waiting on her. She sat down beside me and drew her plate. We ate in silence and simply enjoyed each other's company like we always do. I think she was trying to process how happy I looked because she couldn't stop sneaking glances at me, and I couldn't stop smiling like a fool.

"I picked your car up, but I got this weird vibe that someone was watching me the whole time."

I looked at her with a puzzled look. "What do you mean? Why do you think that?"

She took a sip of wine and then answered me. "I don't know. I just felt watched. Then when I was driving over here, I could have sworn this black car was following me. I stopped at the light and it stopped beside me, but the windows were really dark, like illegal dark." She looked a little thrown about the car.

"They were probably just going the same direction as you," I said. She was probably just imagining it following her.

"I saw the same car for like four blocks, but maybe you're right. Anyways, tell me about this smile of yours?"

At first, I didn't want to talk about it for fear that all the good things happening lately would vanish, but now I was excited. "So, you already know about the dinner invite?" I started.

"Yes, yes. When you got there, what happened?" she said, all giddy-headed.

94

"He was a sight for sore eyes is what. The restaurant was amazing but him, it's like I was drawn to him. He stood for me when I reached the table. We talked for hours. Apparently he works in some high-profile capacity so he doesn't talk about his job much."

Jess was such an attentive listener. "So he's rich and sexy as hell?" She commented like that didn't describe everyone in this city.

"Not only that, he's caring, he listened to me when I talked, and we talked, for hours. It was like time stood still for us. We talked about everything and nothing." Jess had an apologetic look on her face. When I finished my rant, it didn't sit well with me. It was her mother-hen look.

"Sounds like he played you to get in your pants, honey." I turned away from her.

He didn't play me. "No, he didn't. I, uh, didn't get that impression from him." The more I spoke, the faster my heart pitter-pattered for his closeness. *I missed him already.*

"Did you get his number?"

"Um, we, um, no." I didn't know how to answer.

"Did he get your number?"

"I, ahh, ahm. I don't know."

Damn it, but he didn't play me. He said, he, *damn it*. "Did I get played, Jess?" I guess I had a self-pity look, because her mother-hen, murderous glare turned into the mother-hen smothering plea.

She took my finished glass of wine and sat it on the countertop. "You both got caught up in the moment and had an amazing twenty-four hours together. Now let's forget about Mr. Scrumptious and watch a movie. I shook my head yes, but my mind was far away from a movie night. I constantly poked at the memory of him, of us. Less than four hours ago, he had me laid out on a piano making sweet music to my dangerously obedient body. Now, all I wanted was to fold up in my bed and retrace every step his fingers took on my body. I fell asleep halfway through the movie. When I felt my neck paining me, I stirred awake. Jess was in deep conversation in the kitchen. I knew that from the living room floor because she was pacing the tiles loudly. After rubbing out my neck, I got up and went to bed. The next day I got to the office at 9:30 a.m. I didn't have a client until 11:30, so I took my time. When I got there, I had a delivery from him.

I really enjoyed our impromptu day together. Strangely, I never took your number. Mine is 876-712-2112. I'll be waiting by the phone for your call just so you know.

96

Help save the world by saving me. Call me. - Vinte Sanchez

After the night I had debating if I was played, yes or no, I took my phone out so fast I was dialing the number before I knew it. He picked up on the second ring and I was so excited to call that I didn't plan anything to say other than "Hi." It was almost a squeal.

"Hi, gorgeous," he replied.

"Thank you for the flowers. They smell so good," I said while playing with my little ponytail.

"You're welcome. Consider them an apology for not asking for your number when I really wanted it."

My subconscious had to poke the bear and ask the next question. "Oh, so is it that you no longer wanted my number?" Jess was in my head again, singing "He played you" on repeat.

"Oh, no. I didn't mean it like that, love. I just meant that I should have asked sooner, that's all." He had a way with words, simple but effective.

"Okay, so, um, what now?" I was really out of my element here. I had never been in a relationship before. Was this even a relationship?

"Now we get to know each other, not just our anatomy."

Mmmhm. I think I liked the sound of this.

"I'll bite. What do you want to know?" At this point my heels were scrapping the top of my desk, my handbag somewhere on the floor, and I was lost in him.

"I want to know everything."

Lord, the only other person to know everything was Jess. "I love the color blue, am turning twenty-one in a couple weeks, and I graduated with honors early," I smiled to myself, feeling satisfied.

Then I heard the tastiest laughter coming through the speakerphone, casting a smile on my own lips. "Terriana, I want to know about you, not the things I could find on your Facebook."

Well, what else was there to tell? "Help me out then. I don't know what to say," which was the truth. People talk to me, not the other way around. I was used to listening.

"Did you always want to be a psychologist?" He wanted to know about work, okay.

"I didn't know what I wanted to do when I grew up. I just wanted to grow up really, to live that long." Gosh! The line was silent. I knew he was there, I could hear him breathing.

"Why wouldn't you live that long?"

I was kind of hoping he wouldn't ask that, wishful thinking and all. "The short version, my mom was never there. When she finally died, it was like burying a stranger at eleven. Dad fell off the wagon right after and pretty much left me for dead. Everything I have I owe to Jess, including my life."

Wasn't that embarrassing? I could hear him breathing and the wheels in his head turning. I didn't want or need his pity. I had enough for a lifetime. "Am sorry life hasn't been kind to you. I guess, in a way, we're more alike than we thought. My stepdad used to beat on my mom, and she used to take it out on me, until I stopped it. Now am pretty much on my own. My grandma was my hero growing up. I owe all my success to her," he said, a little more to himself than to me, I gathered, but I liked the transparency.

"What do you do for a living?" I guess I wasn't as okay with his vague answer from our dinner after all.

"I work in law enforcement," he said with a smile in his voice.

"Was that so hard to tell me all this time?" Oh, am getting bold. I smiled to myself.

"No, it wasn't hard. I just can't get into any further details is all." He was smirking now. I could feel it.

99

"Like a detective?" Oh, you were sure pushing now.

"Terriana," my name sounded good on his tongue. He knew what he was doing saying it too.

"Yes?" I felt a little tension between my thighs.

"I'm going to spank you next time I see you, which will be tonight, for a little dinner date, if you'd have me?" How could a girl say no to that?

"It's Monday. What did you have in mind?" I didn't know much about the restaurant scene in this city. I tried to avoid spending money as best as possible.

"I know a small place a little at the border. I'll pick you up. What time will you be finished working?"

Oh, snap. It was 11:30. I had a client coming now. "Um, I finish at six." I rushed out.

"I'll see you at six then. I can't wait to spank you." He laughed at the ending, too amused with himself. Before I could reply, I heard a tap at the door.

Crap!

"Just a second, please," I shouted. "I have to go. My first client is here." I really didn't want to hang up.

"I thought I was your first client?" he said, all flirty.

"Are you saying something is mentally wrong with you?" I teased.

100

"Yes, am oddly falling for a stranger I've known less than a week."

Oh.my.God. Mr. Scrumptious just turned Mr. Bold. "I, um, I don't know what to say," I whispered out.

"Enjoy your day, gorgeous. We'll talk later. Go meet with your client." He didn't sound put off by my lack of a reply.

"Okay, talk later. Bye," I said half mindedly.

"Later," he said. Then he was gone.

It took me a couple more minutes to gather myself, but my client didn't seem to mind the wait at all. The day ran off smoothly. My clients talked, and I listened and gave my input when needed. When my last session wrapped up at 5:30, I took fifteen minutes to freshen up a bit, just to look more presentable. It was a blessing in disguise when I found this three-piece suit in my closet. Without the blazer, it showed a peak of my stomach and my upper back. I paired it with black heels and a cute handbag. Orange wasn't one of my favorites, but it complemented my skin tone well.

The next fifteen minutes was spent consulting my bestie. I needed her to calm me down and tell me what to do. "So, he called. Well, he sent me flowers with his number, so I called," I blapped out before she could properly open the line.

"Oh, he called? Well, you, whatever. You guys talked on the phone. Perfect." She said mockingly.

"So does that mean he isn't playing me?" The only question I needed answering.

"It means he is interested, which is great. You deserve someone other than me in your life," she replied truthfully.

"But do I deserve him though, Jess?" I was a bit apprehensive.

"Honey, you deserve the world. The question is, does he deserve to be in your world?" I smiled. I really needed her tonight.

"He asked me out again, tonight," I was super excited at this point, butterflies and all.

"That's so fast though," she said, probably mad she won't get to doll me up, but I felt good in what I was wearing.

"I know. Isn't it exciting, besides you go out all the time." She laughed at my reply.

"Touché. I guess you're a big girl now. Have fun, not too much fun though," she mother 'hened.'

"Yes, mum," I mocked. I motioned at my watch and read five minutes to six; ample time to lock up the office and head downstairs.

"Later, chica. Text you later," I said.

"Adios me amore," she replied, flexing her travel gains.

I made my way into the lobby and stood waiting for him; five minutes turned into twenty. Twenty minutes turned into an hour, before I knew it, I was sitting staring out the glass door. I called him three times, all voicemail. I texted him five times but no reply. I could have sworn he said tonight. I was sure I didn't dream up the whole conversation, besides he wasn't returning any of my calls.

Six o'clock turned into nine thirty way faster than I realized. I peeled my broken pride and spirit off the bench I was on and dragged myself out of the office building to my car. The only sound I could hear were my heels clinking away and the harshness of the wind. I should have brought my blazer. So much for looking cute for him.

Sigh.

With my head down, I slid into Merci and locked the doors, threw my bag on the passenger side, and let my emotions take over.

Stupid.stupid.stupid.

Maybe he got caught up at work or he lost his phone or something. I didn't bother going over to Jess'. I went home and took a bubble bath.

The week ran off, and no word from Mr. Bold. It was as if he was a figment of my imagination. I sat in the lobby for an hour every evening that week, hoping he would show up. I didn't know how to get to his house. I had only been there once, and I was distracted the whole drive. Plus, it seemed borderline stalker to show up unannounced at someone's house.

KNOCK, KNOCK, KNOCK.

"It's open," I said. I knew who it was anyway.

"What's going on, Terri?" Jess asked, plopping down on my bed. It was Saturday evening, a little after three. I went to the office this morning. After my client's sessions, I came back, drank some wine, and curled up in bed ever since playing Sinead Harnett on repeat.

"He left," was all I said, muffled by my pillows.

"When?" She said, puzzled.

104

"He never showed up for our date, and he hasn't been returning my calls."

The room was silent. The song ended and was about to start up again. "You're not making any sense, dear. Get up and talk to me!" She shouted, pulling at the sheets.

"No," I whimpered.

"Get up!" She yelled over the music.

"Hey, stop yelling at me," I deadpanned while turning to her with a flare.

"You didn't show up for tea this morning. I even sent Sarah to your office, and she said you weren't there. Talk to me, and turn that shit down. No one died," she bellowed, but something did die, *my heart*.

I shuffled for the remote under my pillow and turned it down reluctantly. "Thank you. Now please tell me you didn't full his inbox?"

I looked down, guilty as fuck. *Sigh*.

"Now he probably thinks you're crazy," she squinted her eyes at me.

"I didn't know what else to do. I don't know where he works. I can't remember his address, and he is getting my messages and not replying to them. He left me on read, for crying out loud," my self-pity transformed into anger. Why do people always just leave? No note, no

105

apology, they just up and walk out of my life. I didn't realize I had been crying until I felt Jess running her fingers through my hair, cooing me like a baby. I thought I was broken until now. All this time I was whole.

Sigh! He broke me.

Chapter 10
Vinte

"How is she?" Every time I asked this question, I felt a little part of me hating myself a little more. I had never regretted anything in my life, but the moment my boss signaled that he needed a word when I was talking to her, I regretted never being a little bolder.

"She waited in the lobby again, cried in her car again, then she went home. She hasn't come out since."

If I could take back that first night, I would. It was selfish of me to approach her in the first place.

"Are you still there?" Jay asked.

I was reeling in my inner monologue. "Yea, am just wondering how I'm going to fix this or if I can. I practically walked out of her life the moment she gave me a reason not to." I get why she opened up to me, she was tired of holding out on life. She was begging for me to be different. I've probably pushed her mentally over the edge.

107

"She was abandoned by everyone who was supposed to stick by her, and here I am, miles away and I couldn't even tell her why." I said, totally defeated.

"We protect and serve. One day she'll understand if she's the one. Man up." Naejay might be a girl, but her favorite line is 'man up;' classy until her last day.

"If someone completely walked out of your life and couldn't tell you they were enlisted for a private need to know detail, in less words, would you believe them? Keep in mind that you knew them for not even two days?" Situation-ships like these are why I didn't date.

"No, but she isn't me. You can't declare yourself a failure if you haven't at least tried. Now get off the line and back to work. The pity party is over." She hung up. I smirked to myself. If there was a bet who was in the army, me or Jay, am sure I would be rich from people's wrong answers.

It had been a week since that dreaded day. It started out so good though. I made a reservation and had a whole evening planned out. Looking back at it now, to be honest, I didn't know what came over me. I planned dinner and a stroll on a beach with the intention of getting her back into my bed. I couldn't get enough of her, and I knew she wouldn't say no. I could feel her fondness for me.

108

We had only spent a day together, but that was all it took. When I finally went to work, I was hauled up in the break room, trying to be out of sight while I spoke to her. The precinct was huge, yes, but cops walked in and out so often, it was hard to have a moment of privacy. When my boss spotted me, smiling from ear to ear, mug in my hand and love in my eyes, I was done for. With a finger pointed dead at me, then flexed in that 'come' sign, I knew I wouldn't like what was *coming*.

I was last to enter the captain's office. Upon entering, I saw Jay, Sammie, the other guys, the FBI director and their best agent, Billy. '*The fuck is going on now*' was the only thing I had on my mind at this time. I stepped in and Jay gave me a look, and all shit broke loose after that: Covert mission across the world, gathering intel with Billy on an offshore terrorist group, with the intent of fumbling their attack. The more information we unearthed, the more I wanted to go home, not because the terrorist were making strategic plays but because this mission didn't need me across the world; something just wasn't adding up.

There were eight terrorists; two were females. They all had a similar history though: military rejects dishonorable leave. The odd thing was, none of them did a tour with each other. Their ages ranged between twenty-three and forty-five. They all originated from

109

different parts of the world, so how did they meet? What was the common denominator? Their leader went by the name Bell. There was no record or paper trail of this man existing, so how did we even get wind of the group in the first place? This CIA alien was known for everything smuggling related, from babies to missiles, so when did he upgrade to terrorism? All these unanswered questions, and we had been on their ass for almost a year. They hadn't made a move in that whole time; just planning something big. With the amount of ammunition he had, he could arm the whole of New York City with ease.

The group had eight different criminal personalities infused in them also: the gunslinger, psychotic, bomb expert, technician, getaway expert, chameleon, hijacker, and kidnapper. They could be planning a number of different crimes simply based on their known skills, but which was the most dominant right now? Their last threat that brought me here over a month ago was inciting the war between the drug cartels, which led to my last buss. I guess I should really be thanking them for stirring the pot, but why?

Chapter 11
Terriana

I didn't know if it was paranoia or plain crazy, but I had been feeling followed for the last couple of weeks. At first, I thought it was him. I was dumbly hoping he was there whenever I turned around, but he never was. It had been almost a month since Vinte Sanchez waltzed in and out of my life like a tornado. I got hot flashes thinking about him. I wake moaning his name, then get frustrated when I wake with my hand between my thighs; *how embarrassing, right?* But, each step I trotted today has been mimicked. I looked ahead in the store windows trying to make out who had been following me. Then I saw my chance: the Prada store just added a revolving door to one of their corner stores. If I could slip in, I could end up behind whoever was trailing me. I paced myself and executed perfectly, if I do say so myself. I followed the door around, and through the glass doors I could see the confusion on her face. *She fucked up, and she knew it.*

"Why have you been following me?" I shrieked out instantly with one hand in my bag holding my pepper spray.

"Am not following you, miss," she replied calmly. *Too calm.*

"Liar!" She squinted her eyes at me. "You twitched your hand when you said you're not following me. Now, let's try this again. Why are you following me?"

She was contemplating something, like getting caught wasn't a factor. The look on her face was so telling; amateur poker player. "Vinte needed you safe while he is out of town."

I think that was when my world shattered. He *needed* me safe—the nerve of him. "Are you kidding me? He left me in the lobby with no apology, no explanation but sends you to trail my ass like a stalker." I tempered out, clutching my pepper spray for dear life.

"Am sorry about that. He is too. He had no time to reach out to you, and he regrets it."

Well, I have no time to care. "Well, fuck him. Stop following me." I turned on my heels and ran to the bus I was eyeing for the last two minutes. I got on, and she tried catching it but failed miserably. I suppose she was not expecting it at all. Merci was getting a check-up at the garage around the corner from my office, but I didn't mind taking the bus. They used to be one of the few times I stayed warm. The bus ride was peaceful; the bus stop was approximately a twenty-minute walk from my apartment. I haven't needed to do this in a long time. I began the short walk, and it was like déjà vu again.

"Are you seriously following me still?" I whisper yelled, but no reply. I turned around and nothing or no one, I should say. I rounded the corner leading to my apartment and heard footsteps again. It was seven at night, but it was fairly light out still. I looked over my shoulder and saw no one again. I stopped shy of my apartment and did a full scan of the area. I couldn't see anyone behind me. I heard a vehicle in the direction of my apartment and turned with speed in the same direction. The vehicle approaching seemed like a jeep with really bright headlights. I turned towards my building, and the footsteps came at me so fast it was like the wind got knocked out of me, arms wrapped around my waist, and a bag pulled over my head. My 'taken' instinct chipped in. I yelled, screamed, and swung like crazy. Car tires squeaked, clicking sounds, I was thrown on some seats. A hand held my head, and something was pushed into my neck, then I was out.

I woke up to girls whispering. "She looks young."

113

"Poor baby."

"Hopefully she doesn't get herself killed."

"Let's pray she isn't a fighter."

"Do you see those manicured nails and her clothes?"

"Yeah, she is a goodie too shoe."

"Mhmm." My head was throbbing and I needed them to shut up, then I remembered that I didn't have roommates. The bed was hard and cold. I didn't remember getting home. I did remember feeling followed, being thrown in a car, manhandled, and subconsciously poked and prodded. I flew up so fast my head spun. Six pairs of eyes looked at me with sympathy. We were in a mesh cage like something out of the Teen Wolf series. They looked pale, a little dusty, more than likely from sleeping on the ground—this ground with each girl having a space of their own and not huddled together. "Where am I? Where are we?" I stuttered out. My throat was dry, and I felt under dressed, but that was just how I felt, not how I actually was. "Where am I?" I hushed out.

I didn't even know why I asked. Shock, cold, and soulless eyes stared at me. As they rattled on, trying to catch me up, the only thing that stuck were the words 'kidnapped' and 'sex trafficking.' By the time the red head's lips stopped moving, I ran so fast as If I could go anywhere. "Let me out. Help! Let me out! Let me out! Let me out!" I screamed and shook the mesh vigorously. I felt tiny hands pulling at me, screaming at me to 'shut up,' 'don't make them angry,' don't this, don't that. I screamed for help so long and so loud, my face was drenched from tears and my body was shaking from adrenaline. I felt like a caged bird. I had slept in enough jail cells to hate the site of this death trap I was thrown in. "Help!" I screamed for the life of me.

"This one is a screamer," I heard a voice chime in from a stairwell I didn't notice before.

Where the hell am I?

I heard muffled talking and watched as someone walked forward into the light.

"Fuck!" the woman said. She sounded so familiar. She stopped just shy of the light on her face. I could only see her chest down. Absolutely not what I was expecting. Instead of seeing leather jackets or punk rock shoes or something more badass, I saw manicured nails, pencil skirt, blazer jacket, and the tips of honey-blond hair, but I couldn't get her voice out of my head. It was like a blast from the past.

Where the hell am I, and why does this woman sound like...

115

"Who brought her here?" the woman said to the men gawking from behind her. Unlike her, they didn't avoid the lights from the broken lampshade in this musty basement.

"Jackson and his guys, ma'am," one of the men said.

"Why the hell am I here? Let me out!" I screamed and punched the cage. I didn't even realise that the other girls were huddled together to the rear of the cage against the wall, hiding their faces.

"Someone get Bell on the line. Jackson fucked up!" I knew that voice. I halted all movement trying to adjust my eyes to make her face out, but she spun on her heels too quickly, so I just went for it.

"Victoria!" I screamed through the darkness.

She stopped in her tracks, and I could make out her silhouette looking over her shoulder at me. "See you soon, Bluebell."

Bitch!

She continued walking away from me. "Victoria!" I screamed, but nothing changed. "Victoria, get me out of here. Help! Victoria. Victoria!" I broke out in tears, snot running and fist-bruising tears. I kicked, I yelled, and hit the cage like a crazy person.

116

"How do you know her?" a voice said as tiny arms wrapped around me.

"My stepmother." I heard gasps and felt judgmental eyes on me. I sat with my back on the mesh of the cage and stared at the girls. "My name is Terriana. We might as well be on first-name basis after all." They looked at me as if I was a piece of gum under their shoe; ironic considering I was the only one still wearing shoes. They were stripped down to their underwear, and each had a dirty blanket tethered to them. In the brief minutes that I met and ran from Vinte's friend, I prayed to God she saw something because I had no one else to be hopeful to.

"Maci." a girl said, breaking me out of my daydream.

"I'm Lena. That's Tory, Bree, Miya, and Camiel." The girl that hugged me said with a weak smile.

"So what now?" A girl asked, tears in her eyes and shivering. I took my jacket off and threw it over her shoulders, with the dust from the concrete floor ascending around the tail of the coat.

"I don't know, but am positive we're going to get the hell out of here." I vowed.

The door rattled open at the top of the stairwell. Several heavy footsteps descended. One of the five men I counted stepped forward. I got up and turned to him, ready for anything. He stepped towards the cage, and I stepped back towards the other girls. He swept his eyes over us and stepped inside. "You," he pointed at Miya.

"What do you want with her?" I breathed far too quickly. He grabbed her by the wrist and pulled her up. I grabbed her other arm in a vice grip. "Hey!" I screamed.

"Wait your turn!" he replied, pushing me into the arms of the other quivering girls. By the time I got my footing in check, the cage closed, and Miya was screaming tears and being dragged by her hair.

"Why the fuck did you guys just stand there and let him take her!" They were crying like cowards and shaking, rubbing their bodies, and looking everywhere but at me.

"They know better than to fight my men by now. They've been here a couple of days, but they're a quick study this group." He said.

I looked across the room, anticipating the site of the man I hadn't seen in what, six years, soon seven. He stepped into the light, and I saw that he hadn't aged a day, but the once feeble, once dazed allure he had was gone, replaced by something disturbed. He had a calculated look about him. Looking at the suit-clad man that loomed over me by at least six inches, I felt perturbed. So many questions floated around in my head,

118

from '*Where have you been?*' to '*Why did you leave me?*' But none of that mattered. If I was kidnapped along with six other girls, trapped in a cage in a basement like something off Chicago PD, what he had to say wasn't what I hoped to hear. Then the question surged, '*What did I want to hear?*' He left me to go start a new life; he was in rehab all this time. For the past six years, I had been praying he was dead. Maybe this was my karma for wishing death on another. I wanted to scream at him, run Merci over him, but I couldn't.

"Hi, Bell." I said.

"Where did my little Bluebell go? No, 'Hi, dad?'"

Chapter 12
Vinte

"Fuck, I've been calling you. I'm headed home from the airport." I said to Jay's open line.

"I fucked up," she whimpered out.

"Where is she?" I said as calmly as humanly possible.

"She was kidnapped," my grip tightened around the steering wheel, and my foot got a little heavier on the gas.

"Naejay, quit fucking with me," I said it, but my body said otherwise. My heart was racing a mile a minute. My brain was sieving through past events, and I was rattled like a lion in a cage.

"She made me. I don't know how, but the girl is smarter than she lets on. She made me and called me out on it too like a human lie detector. She slipped away on a bus because her car was in the shop. By the time I got to her apartment, men were throwing her into a jeep. I followed them for ten blocks, and then they vanished." She was panting like crazy, and I knew she was already beating herself up about it; no need to add insult to injury.

"How long?" depending on why she was taken, there is a certain time period in saving her.

"Seven hours. I'm at her loft at Buckhead, since she was taken from here."

She hadn't invited me over as yet. We hadn't reached that far, and now this. "I'm on my way."

I got to the apartment so fast I had to look up and down the street twice to double-check check I didn't hit anyone. I didn't bother to wait for the elevator. I needed to calm my nerves, so I climbed the stairwell two at a time. I knew where she lived and her apartment number from the day I left her at the coffee shop seducing me with her eyes. I knocked twice, and Jay opened the door and stepped aside. Surveillance from outside was rolling. Her living room looked like a quiet storm had whipped through it, and Jay was doing the second thing she did best, hacking.

I called her Jay because that was her hacker name before she joined the force. With a demanding job like ours, individuality was important so you didn't lose yourself. "This guy here, I didn't realize at first, but he has an invisible tattoo on his arm. When I double-checked the other guys that are caught in frame, I found that they had the same tattoos. I wouldn't have seen it if her light was normal, worse because it's a video." I looked down on the screen and at the tattoo. "Am cross-checking it into our database to see if I get a match." Yes, that was illegal, but who gave a fuck right now. I needed her found and no hair out of place on her head.

"What did you mean the jeep vanished?" I asked her.

"We were on fifth and twenty-seventh street. They rounded the corner, went under the bridge, and I was the only one that came out. I searched the area and saw no way how a big ass jeep could have just up and vanished."

We were waiting on her search to come back, and I was itching to search her things but being there felt wrong. "We're wasting time here. We need to go into the office with what we have and get more eyes on the ground. She could be halfway around the fucking world by now." I think the severity of the situation was just catching up on me.

"We have the kidnapping on video. We don't need to wait twenty-four hours. Besides, my rank and relationship or lack thereof should be enough."

We heard someone approaching the door. I pulled my gun out along with Jay. Keys rattled so I flicked the light off and Jay pushed the laptop face down. The door clicked open and Jessica's voice filled the room. "Terri, where the fuck are you?" she screamed, slamming the door shut behind her and moving across the living space not bothering to turn on a light.

"Jess," I said, trying not to spook her. Oh boy, did I fail. I was behind her, so she swung around knocking me upside the head while screaming and throwing some heavy punches. Jay turned the lights on while I tried blocking Jessica's blows. "Hey, hey, hey. It's just me. Hey!" I had her back pinned to my front and her hands clad in mine trying to steady her. She looked over her shoulder, and her face went from angry to bat-shit crazy.

"You motherfucking piece of shit." She said, swinging out of my grip. "You left without a word, and you broke her. What the fuck are you doing in here, and who the fuck is this bitch?" she screamed like she was trying to wake up the whole damn block. "Shhhh. I know I fucked up. Am sorry, but we don't have time for this. Someone took Terri." I shouted over her rant.

"What?" she whisper yelled, all signs of rage transformed into deep worry. "What do you mean someone took her?" she yelled with a murderous stare.

"That's what we're trying to figure out. Jay lost her, and someone took her." I said with a hint of annoyance.

"Hey, I wouldn't have lost her if she didn't run." Jay countered from her computer screen.

124

"I still don't get how she even made you. You're an undercover cop for fuck's sake." I said way too angrily, because I knew there must have been a really good reason she lost *her*.

"What the fuck is going on here? Somebody explain, and I mean now?" Jess shouted with her knocks turning white.

"I had to leave and I wasn't given a chance to tell Terri. Jay was supposed to watch her-"

"I did watch her," Jay interrupted.

"…but Terri made Jay and ran. By the time Jay got here, someone was hauling her off in a jeep, and they disappeared a couple blocks away from here." I said, mentally prepared for a fight.

"You're like CIA or some shit?" she asked. Maybe I wasn't expecting that.

"Or some shit?" I replied.

"I got something," Jay said from behind us.

We both shuffled over to Jay, staring at the screen. "Is that an underground sewer line?" I asked, pointing at the screen.

"Yes," Jay said simply while still typing away.

125

"What does it mean though?" Jess asked with her arms folded moving from left to right on the spot.

"It means that they didn't disappear. They went underground, I think." Jay said more to herself than to us.

"What do you mean 'you think?'" Jess stopped rocking and yelled at Jay.

"Aaah, stop yelling in my ear, for fuck's sake." Jay reprimanded Jess.

"We're wasting time. We need to go into the office and get back up." I said.

"I don't know why you didn't call the cops in the first place. Let's go. Someone could be trying to kill my best friend, and you two morons are doing nothing." Jess said while marching out the door. Jay and I both looked at each other, and she shook her head at me while packing up her gear. By the time we got downstairs, Jess was turning around on the road. Jay and I got into our vehicles and followed her. We got to an intersection and pulled up beside Jess and told her to follow us. She was headed to the local precinct but that was not where we were going.

We pulled into the underground parking lot, and Jay and I got out of our vehicles at the same time. Walking

126

to the elevator, I realised that Jess was still in her car and she parked further from ours. "What's she waiting on? An invitation?" Jay asked, still aiming for the elevator.

"She doesn't know us. Her best friend was taken, and she's scared. I'll meet you up there. Brief the others." I said, walking over to Jess' car. I pulled my ID out and put it up against the glass of her window. She looked down at it and opened her door and stepped out.

"Why would someone take her? She barely knows you. You went on one date?" she said with tears in her eyes.

"I don't know. Did she say anything at all to you that just seem off or bizarre or anything?" I asked her, holding her shoulders reassuringly.

"I don't know. She just felt like someone was following her is all," she said, shaking her head.

"That might have been Jay. Let's go up and see what we can find."

We started walking to the elevator. I could see how lost Jess was right now, and she looked like she could snap at any minute. "We're going to find her," I said as the elevator opened.

"You better find her if you know what's good for you!" she deadpanned.

I really couldn't blame her. It was my fault someone took her, but who? I had so many cases.

We rode up to CIA headquarters in silence. As the door opened, all eyes fell on us. "She wants to see you. I'll watch her." Jay said with an apologetic glance at me.

Knock, Knock.

I walked in and saw my boss, Natalia Clark, staring at her computer screen. She signaled for me to sit, and I did. "Why the fuck did you take so long to come in with this?" she barked at me.

"I just got back in town, and we don't know if it's related to me or not," I said.

"We assume the worst and work from there. Does she know about you?" she asked.

So that is her concern.

"No, she doesn't know am CIA," I answered.

"But she assumes something?" she rebutted.

"Possibly. I had Jay tailing her and she made her," I said, looking everywhere but at Natalie.

"She did what now," She said, looking at me over her glasses. "How?"

128

"That's what I said," I replied. "Her mom was a marine, but she died years ago, so it's hard to say," I added.

"Well, go see what the team found and keep me posted."

I got up and out of her office and headed straight for our team's office. When I walked in, it was chaotic. Jay and Jess were going at it while Sam was playing referee. "She was being followed before his dumb ass met her," Jess said.

"He was watching her before he approached her," Jay said.

"So, who moved her car then? Who sent her flowers in the hospital? Someone has been watching her for years?" Jess said.

"She was probably just paranoid. She's young and lived alone," Jay said.

"No, she wasn't. I don't even know why..." she started saying, but I cut her off.

"Which flowers?" I asked Jess.

"She was attacked from a robbery at my coffee shop a couple of months ago. I just got back in town from my trip the day she got out of the hospital. I went to the hospital where she was supposed to be but all that was there were flowers signed 'D'," She said to me, with her hands folded. "But that's not even the weird part. Someone drove her car from the parking lot of her office to the hospital, directly in front of the emergency door. She said she had asked you, and you said it wasn't you, so who was it? I was out of town." She looked worried and frustrated as any friend would be; they were like sisters after all.

"Sounds like she has a stalker to me. Does she have any ex with an initial 'D'?" I asked.

"She's never dated before you, if we can even call it that. You bailed before anything," she said. I guess I deserved that last jab. "And, no, you weren't her first," she added. I guess my face gave it away because I was also reveling in that little bit of information.

"Fuck," Sam said from across the room.

"What you found?" I asked, sauntering over to him.

He turned the screen around, and everyone reacted the same.

"FUCKK!"

Wait, Jess.

"You know this man?" I probed her, pointing to the monitor.

130

"Well, he looks a little older, but that's Terri's dad," she replied a little confused.

"Fuck. 'D' isn't an initial, it means Dad," Jay said.

"So this just moved from a kidnapping to a possible terrorist attack," Natalia said from behind, surprising everyone.

"Jessica Parkins, right?" Natalia continued.

"Yes, that's me," Jess replied nervously.

"Your friend's father is on the US most wanted terrorist list. What's his name? We only have an alias. We need to know everything you know about him. Times ticking, and we don't know what he wants with Terriana," Natalia declared, using Jess' need to find Terri as a ploy for another huge buss. The room went silent as everyone looked at Jess. I hated putting her on the spot, but I needed Terri, and her father was a fucking sociopath. Strange how Terri became a psychologist.

"Jess, take your time. Anything you say could be useful," I said, trying to calm her nerves.

"That almost sounded like you were going to read me my rights," she squeaked nervously.

"No, you haven't done anything wrong so why would we?" I laughed, trying to lighten the atmosphere.

"His name is James Bell. She hasn't seen him in over six years when he got married to a woman he met at a bar. Her name is Victoria something, Mercy or Michael or something. Her mom was Narriana Bell. Died somewhere on duty. She was a marine. Terri lived on the streets for years until I found her. What I never told her was that her dad came looking for her once," she said, twiddling with her hands nervously.

"What do you mean once? What happened?" I probed.

"He showed up at my apartment after three in the morning, but she didn't tell me about him yet. I didn't know what he looked like. I never opened the door. I just saw him through the peephole of my door, but he had bad news written all over him. He told me who he was, but she was in a bad place. I couldn't have him fuck her up worse, so I told him she was dead, and it looked like he believed." She had regret plastered on her face.

"A man like Bell would have checked or something."

"You're forgetting who I am. My grandfather is Carter Pearrie," she said like it was nothing.

"Your grandfather is the head of the fucking CIA?" I yelled.

"That's why you stopped downstairs?" Jay added as shocked as I was.

"Your grandfather wants to see you. He said you should stop by when you're finished here," Natalia said, nonchalantly looking at me.

"You knew about this?" I asked Natalia.

"I'm CIA," she replied, like that magically fucking explained everything. "Sam, have you found her yet?" Natalia was completely ignoring my 'What the fuck look'.

"Call me when there's news. I have to go," Jess said, picking up her things.

"Secret service will escort you to your grandfather," Natalia told Jess, grabbing her hand on the way out.

"Seriously, am not twelve. I can take care of myself now!" Jess shouted, completely pissed as she stormed out with security tailing her.

"Somebody explain what's going on?" I demanded, staring at Natalia.

"Jessica comes from a long line of CIA on her father's side, so when her mother kicked her out and her grandfather started funding everything and assigned secret service to watch her, she got curious like every teenager and figured it out. The deal was she lives a normal life, but she wears a tracking device. Jessica gave Terriana the tracking device because she used to sleepwalk. So, her dad had two made since he naturally gained two granddaughters. Fill in the blank," she deadpanned.

How the fuck did I miss all this. I did a background check for crying out loud.

"Shit! When I did the background check on Terri, that's how Bell found her," I said like the smartest fool in the room.

"Thanks for catching up Special Agent Sanchez," Natalia snided.

I really wanted to tell her to go fuck herself, but I actually liked my job and should wait until I found my girl.

"Bell seems to have a frequency blocker because it's not giving us a direct location," Sam said from his desk by the door.

Peep. Peep.

"Got him!" Sam shouted.

"Let's go!" I said to Jay. I grabbed two guns and my knives and fastened them on me.

"I need Bell dead or alive. I don't care," Natalia said.

134

"Fine by me," I smirked.

As we made our way down the elevator, I checked my phone for any signs of life. I didn't know if I expected her to call or I expected a ransom note. I kept praying he didn't hurt her, and then I remembered the man I had been watching for the last month was her damn father, a damn terrorist, human trafficker. I just hope he was being a father.

Chapter 13
Terriana

The man I once thought I knew had five girls in a cell, cold, hungry, and exposed in front of his men like meat on a platter. He observed me as if his brain was trying to register the daughter he once abandoned. "You dyed your hair," he said, matter of fact like. No question about it. I could hear the girls whimpering away behind me, still huddled together for warmth, like wolves in a pack.

"Shortly after coming off the streets," I replied, completely aware that he was using small talk to psychoanalyze me. "You would know if you ever bothered looking for me." I chuckled to myself mostly.

"I see you're still the stupid naive girl you always were." he replied, completely void of any emotions. I guess the alcohol didn't make him bitter, I just met the real him drunk. "How is that friend of yours, Jessica is it?" he beamed with a mischievous grin.

"How the hell do you know Jessica?" I blurted out, getting my bearings in check before getting on my feet.

"I came for you once. She said you were dead. I did some checking just to add the final nail in the coffin, and the report said you died in a car accident," he said, flexing his muscles and gripping the cage looming over me.

"What accident?" I ask stupefied.

"It doesn't matter now. Thanks to whoever ran a background check on you, it was easy pickings finding you again. After all, I can't be America's most wanted and have you fucking it up for me again now can I?" His voice was shrill and his knuckles flexed bone white.

"What do you mean 'again?'"

Fuck! America's Most Wanted? What has he been up to? It's been six whole years. What could he have been doing in that time in addition to kidnapping and sex trafficking?

"Someone get her out of there and bring her to her last room," he said to the room at large.

Out of nowhere, I saw four men approaching.

Have they been there the whole time?

I stepped back from the cage towards the girls. I heard gasps and screams, none for me, all begging not to be harmed. "Get off me!" I screamed as one of the tall, muscular men grabbed my wrist, yanking my body towards him. "Get off me! Let me go!" I shouted, to no prevail.

138

"Always so melodramatic," I heard my father saying, as if his daughter wasn't being manhandled by his own goons. The next thing I knew a cloth was being shoved over my nose and mouth by another goon. I tried to scream, but my voice got trapped in the cloth, and the room spun until my eyelids got heavy then closed.

I felt the sun pelting my flesh before anything else. I woke in a fright and thrust forward with my eyes wide awake. I ran my hands over my body to see if anything was out of place or sore. The man who raised me was long dead, and I had to be ready for anything. Who knew that all those idle self-defense lessons Jess signed us up for as cardio workout would one day come in handy? I haven't gotten my chance yet, but so help me God, I was not going out without a fight.

Wait, my hands are free!

I pulled the covers back and stepped out of the bed to assess my surroundings. No visible cameras, the door was probably closed.

The windows.

I raced to the windows and took in the padlocks that were on them. *Shit.* There was a dresser with a mirror

139

and, what do we have here, a hairbrush with a mirror on the back. *Perfect.* I picked up the hairbrush and tossed it on the bed, then I headed for the closet. How cute he stocked it! Pants, tights, dresses, even shoes in three different sizes. Was he expecting more girls, or he didn't know my size? That or this room was someone else's before mine.

How creepy is that?

I needed as much flexibility as possible if I was going to survive, so I changed. I traded my sheer top for a black fitted tank top, my high waist skirt for black yoga pants, heels for trainers, and I threw on a dark grey jacket. I spotted a couple of belts in the corner of the closet and picked two out, tossing one on the bed along with the brush. I headed back to the dresser, and with a hair tie that was there, I put my hair in a ponytail as best as possible. My hair was showing all its curls having none of my usual products to tame it. If someone saw me now, they would think I was about to go jogging. I took another look out the window. I was on some kind of ranch I didn't recognise. Judging by the look of it, we were miles away from another property, and we were completely surrounded by the woods. I hated the outdoors. I had enough growing up in them if you asked me.

Judging by the looks of it, I was on the second floor. The window was padlocked, which meant no security system if I broke the glass out, and it was not grilled.

Thank God. Think I should try the door first? Okay.

I headed to the bed for the hairbrush. I placed the pillow over it and pressed down hard enough to break the glass. I moved the pillow and searched the shard glass for a large enough piece. I then dunked the pillow out of the pillowcase onto the bed and used the pillowcase to wrap one end of the piece of glass, then wrap it around my good hand like a dagger. Now, I was no pro, but I have watched enough episodes of Pretty Little Liars to know better than to wait around, and I have watched enough prison movies to know how to defend myself.

I wrapped the belt around my other hand and held the buckle in my palms.

Now what?

Should I try the door and take my chances, or should I try to shimmy my ass down a drainpipe and run for the woods?

Drainpipe it was. I was already dressed for a hike, so I might as well. It was strange how I wasn't even hungry, and it looked like the sun was actually beginning to set not rise. I could wait for night, but I didn't know how thick the trees were or where I was going.

141

I zipped the jacket up and readied my stance at the window. It was like they wanted me to run. I was naive, so fuck it. I gripped the stool with my hand with the belt, gave it all I got, and smashed the window out in one go. I heard faint footsteps, but I didn't wait for an invite. I broke the rest of the glass with my foot and shimmied outside. There was a small ledge not large enough to run, but I had no choice. I meekly moved my ass to the next window looking into a different room. There was a girl on the bed. I knocked on the glass. She stirred awake and looked in my direction.

Shit. Fucking Victoria.

I saw her eyebrows tilt up, but I was already moving away by the time she started screaming for the damn guards. *I never liked her.* I just knew she was bad news; miss 'Oh, I love your father, dear.' I guess joker needed his harlequin.

I needed to get off this God-forsaken house side. I saw a pile of hay a little far out, and I just went for it without even thinking. I landed square on my ass, but the hay broke my fall. By the time I got up to run, I felt a scalp-ripping grip to my hair. I spun and just swung. The mirror connected his lower abdomen so quickly, I barely felt when I stabbed him. His grip loosened, and I pushed him off with my other hand and stepped away. "Am so sorry. I, I didn't mean to," I quivered out, staring in disbelief at his open wound oozing with blood. I heard faint shouting and shook off the nerves trying to get my feet to operate.

Bang!

That was all it took. One gunshot and I was gone. I turned and ran for the woods like my life depended on it, *because it did.* My feet hit the ground like the bullet did the air. The wind never felt so good against my skin, the freedom in my lungs, and the cool icy touch of the air on my cheek. When I neared the border of the woods and the open field, I heard him shout, "Run, just like your mother!" Strangest thing I had ever heard.

How could my mother have run from you? She loved her job? She died serving our country, right?

As tears started to prick my eyes, I started weaving through throngs of trees. My mind started to drift to the past; all the suppressed arguments, fights, wads of money hidden in the house, all the guns and ammunition I used to find in my play things. The more I ran, the more another part of my brain I hadn't used in years was unlocked. My mother used to train me to fight, but I always assumed it was because that was who she was. I never realized it was because she feared for me. Every time she left, she had the same look in her eyes. It was never 'I

143

hope I return to see you again.' It was always, 'I hope you're here when I get back.'

Bang!

"Shit!" I whisper yelled, trying not to draw attention to myself. I was so caught up in my mind that I didn't see the log sticking out in the way. The shot sounded distant, but who knew if they knew these woods better than a novice like me.

Bang!

I slipped feet first down a ditch. I felt rocks and branches scrape at my leggings on the tumble down to the base. I landed on my face. I was not sure if I passed out or not, but the hoody now covered my head and I felt heavy, as if something was on top of me. I peeked out my eyes and saw dried leaves. I pushed up off the ground and felt the gravel under my palms pushing into the chard of mirror still tied to my hand. I could hear crickets, and the night sky up above looked dark and desolate; no stars in sight, only a full moon. I turned my upper body to see what was burdening my legs. It was bark, leaves, and rocks; must be from the fall.

I got up slowly, trying to adjust to the darkness for any signs of life, but nothing. I was alone. I clinged to the side of the ditch and pulled myself out, and began to walk discreetly. I was not sure which direction I came from,

144

but I prayed I was not heading in circles. The belt around my hand was gone; only the one I fastened around my waist over my leggings was still attached.

How did my life get here? I was happy, loved by few but loved none the least.

As I trotted to no end, my mind landed on him, the thickness of his abs, the way his biceps flexed under me, how smooth and succulent his lips felt on mine. *God, if I make it out of here, he better have a damn good explanation for it.* What would possess a man who made love to a woman like he was famished and she was his only food supply to just vanish? The way his hands bruised me, how his lips drank all my screams, all my moans, how could he leave? I guess the same way my father did.

No, they're not the same, and you know it.

Damn him.

Even at my worst, my mind still found a way to give him reasonable doubt. I wondered if he knew I was missing.

God, I miss him. I miss Jess.

As my eyes teared up, I saw something about a yard out ahead of me.

Abandoned, broken boards, broken windows, and a stench of death emitted from the vacant shed; perfect for hiding until daybreak. I peeped inside, discerning the shack for anything out of the ordinary. Pushing open the door, I stare inside again, squinting my eyes to get a better look. I stepped inside and the floorboards creaked from lack of maintenance. I found a corner in what appeared to be a sheep house, and curled up for the night. As I unwrapped my mirror masterpiece and held it close to my chest, I leaned back against the building, pulling my knees to the back of my folded hands. I didn't know who was looking for me, but I prayed he would find me. The only thing I wanted to do was get lost in his hazel brown eyes and his soft silky hair. I longed for his skin to be pressed up against mine. As my mind wondered on every inch of his body, I could recall, my body relaxed, and my head fell to my knees. I felt every ache of my muscles. I felt scrapes and bruises I didn't feel before. I felt so drained, yet thinking of him, I felt so alive.

Snap!

I jerked out of my sleep with my mirror hand out to attack and my eyes adjusting to the light seeping in. Whispers and subtle movement caught my eye, and I

146

lunged from my corner, mirror gripped firmly in my hand. "Got her!"

I tried to get out but only ended up in one of my pursuer's strong arms. I didn't even see him.

Fuck.

"Let me go!" I wailed at him. I thrashed at his back that I was thrown over, and I screamed. I landed punches, but nothing seemed to even get a reaction out of the muscular beast. After a while, I got so tired and disoriented from being upside down and trying to break free, I think I passed out.

His lips on my body was heavenly. It was just the way his fingers dung into my flesh like a deep tissue massage with a slice of him to add. The way he stared at me the morning after, like I was his world wrapped around him on his bed. I had never done anything like that before, but I wanted him so bad, and his actions spoke volumes because he wanted me just as fucking bad.

When he introduced me as his girlfriend, I was freaked out inside. I was weighing the 'is he crazy' or just stroking my ego after the crazy night we had. No man had every made me orgasm and it felt phenomenal—the way his tongue caressed my folds, how much restraint he had when trying to hold out longer. The way his defined V was taunting me all night, driving in and out of me, the animalistic sounds he made trickled past his lips...

Splash!

I woke with a sputter, coughing up water, *no, gasoline.* Judging by the looks of it, it seemed like I passed out and was revived by a very unnecessary splash to the face. "The fuck!" As I shook my head, trying to clear my hair, I realised I couldn't move my arms. I was tied around the waist with my arms pinned down sitting on the ground.

"You fucked it all up. Ten years of plotting and scheming, all lost. All my guns, all my ammunition was seized by the fucking FBI right in front of my eyes!" he ranted on like the lunatic he obviously had become. Never would I have imagined a reunion with my father would lead to being tied to the same shack I hid from him in, drenched in gasoline.

"What are you talking about? Untie me!" I screamed at him, but it only fell on deaf ears. "Let me go! Help! Help!"

He came near me with a blow torch. "You, can't?" I whimpered, completely thrown. Had it really been so long since I was his little Bluebell? Was I really imagining the affection before he snapped? "Dad!" I screamed at him, trying to break free of the God-forsaken rope.

148

"I haven't been anyone's dad in years, sweetheart," he said to me completely void of any emotions.

Smack!

His fingers imprinted across my face, hard. My jaw clenched and my eyes started to leak the tears that swelled the moment it hit me; I was not getting out of this. No one was coming to save this damsel. "Please, dad. What do you want from me?" I sighed, defeated as ever before.

"Absolutely nothing. I wanted you to join me. Help build my legacy. Help me rid the world of the US riches that think they're better than us," he ranted on again, swinging the torch as if I didn't stink of gas and could light up this little shed like a Christmas tree.

Smack!

His hand connected to my other jaw like a bat would a ball. I screamed in pain and the floodgates completely broke free. "Please!" I wheezed out. My muscles ached. I could feel the rope burns, and my mind did somersaults.

"No one's dying today, love. We just want what we came for, and we'll be on our way, right?"

OMG.

As if my dad slapped some sense into me, I finally realized how dumb I really was. It was him, invading my mind and body and just strangling my soul.

149

Vinte!

He robbed Jess' store, well, the clients in it, and roughed everyone up. *But, that doesn't make sense.* Why would he do that?

"Did you send him to fuck me?" the most revolting question spewed out of my mouth to my once father like a testament of how low I now thought of him.

"Please, don't insult my abilities or blame me for being a little slut like your mother," he spat at me as if I struck a nerve. Vinte said he didn't move my car, so, GOD, I was so confused right now.

"Did you move my car?" I breathed, totally spent from adrenaline and quivering from the cold air that brushed my soaked body.

"You're very easy to stalk, child. I needed to make sure you were really alive. Besides, I needed your address from the GPS," he retorted like the egotistical prick he was.

"So, you've been following me?" I heaved, trying to speak through the massive lump in my throat.

"My men have been tailing you, but kept taking pictures of your friend. You know what they say; want something done right do it yourself," he snided.

150

"Boss, we got to go. They're closing in on us," one of the men from outside shouted.

"Untie me, please!" I said, out of breath and frantic.

He laughed humorlessly at me. "Goodbye, Bluebell." As if the words meant nothing, as if he hadn't walked away six years ago saying those same words, he spun and marched out of the dusty little hut. I screamed so loud, my voice cracked. My eyes stung from crying, and my arms burned from the ropes. The heel of my shoes dug into the broken plyboards that sheeted the floor, and I was slipping on the gasoline. Then I heard the crackles from outside, the stung of smoke in my eyes, and the heat gradually filling the small unit.

"Help!"

Chapter 14
Vinte

I saw the smoke, and I heard her screams a mile away. It sounded like a strangled deer. As I approached the clearing, I mentally prepared for the worst. She had been missing for days now, and even though she shared blood with the maniac, it was not always thicker than water.

"Find Bell!" Natalie barked in my ear. I ripped out my earpiece and charged as close as possible to the doorway her screams echoed out of.

"Terri!" I shouted, trying to see exactly which side she was on.

"In here! Please get me out," she sobbed. A piece of me broke hearing her sound so defenseless.

"Let's try around back!" Jay shouted, suddenly behind me. The moment I heard Terri, I sprinted off not caring for backup. As the others passed us, probably trying to get Bell, Jay and I rounded the corner of the now ablaze building.

"Help!" she cried out. She sounded breathless and panicked. My hands trembled from the fear of losing her. *How could one girl, one momentous night, change my whole life? I was nothing without her, all of her. I.cant.lose.her.*

"Help me!" Jay screamed, jerking me out of my revere. She turned over a water tank on the back of the little shack, outing a substantial area under a broken window. I used my gun to further burst the window in.

She stopped screaming.

"Terri!" I yelled, climbing up on the tank with Jay hoisting me through. As I landed on the ground, one of my feet sunk through the floorboard. As I tugged my feet out, I started coughing up the smoke from the stale air trapped all around. "Terri, wake up!" I shouted, maneuvering over to her. The room was completely white and hot as hell from the slow burning fire that was blazing on the exterior. It felt like a damn oven.

I pulled my knife out of my shoes and cut her free. Pulling her over my shoulder, I carried her towards the window. When I looked outside, trying to see how to get her through, I saw Jay throwing her jacket on the windowsill to make it easier. I eased her down on the window, then pushed her legs through. Her body was limb and immobile. She had to wake up; she just had to.

154

Jay pulled her down, and I climbed through to help her. I took her off Jay who looked like she was about to fall over from Terri's weight. I carried her bridal style away from the havoc happening and laid her down on a patch of grass. "Terri!" I jerked, trying to wake her up, but nothing. Her face was tear stained, red, and swollen, almost discolored like the son of a bitch hit her. "Fuck it!" I pressed my lips to hers pushing air in, then started compression. I had done mouth-to-mouth resuscitation before but never meant it more than today. She tasted and smelt of raw gasoline.

What kind of father would leave his daughter to burn to death?

Her arms had rope burns. Her hair was matted to her face, and she looked exhausted. She fought back. As I swelled with pride knowing that she never gave up, she jolted awake. "Ahh," she said. Her voice strangled trying to gasps for air. She gripped onto me, and my arms wrapped around her protectively.

"Am sorry. I should never have left you. Am sorry." I choked out, emotions washing my whole body as she clinged to me. I ran my fingers up and down her back. She shivered, either from my touch or the cold. I picked her up, held her as tight to my body as possible, planting soft consoling kisses on her forehead as Jay led the way to where the group started the manhunt.

One small tracking device implanted by an unknowing grandfather found a fugitive that had been on the run for over ten years. Bell was almost a CIA operative until he went rogue and tried to flip his own wife, not caring how it would later affect his daughter. He killed his wife and six other marines when he leaked their whereabouts to terrorist, making himself a terrorist of the state. He quickly rose to the Most Wanted list and tried recruiting his daughter thinking she was CIA.

Talk about misunderstandings.

As we got to the clearing of the ranch, medics rushed over to check her over.

As they laid her down, she peeped up at me with a mixture of emotions. "You came looking for me?" She whispered as they rushed her over to the makeshift medical station they had set up. It all happened so fast after that. She was severely dehydrated. Treatment for the rope burns had her heart racing so fast they had to sedate her for the pain. When we arrived at the hospital after not being able to ride in the ambulance, I found Jess there waiting.

We sat in the waiting room in silence while everyone ran around tending to patients. Terri looked so scared, so confused. I think the hardest emotion she gave was betrayal. She looked utterly broken when the captain came and broke down all that had happened. Her father was caught and would be serving the rest of his life in a hole for all his crimes over the years. An investigation into his crimes with his new-found identity also showed that her mother died at his hands. However, she was only wounded by those information. She already knew his story was ugly. The captain told her how her father found her—because of me doing a background check with my CIA resources—and how her father was thrown off for years by her best friend's CIA resources. I watched through the window outside her hospital room as something changed in her eyes. She knew that Jess and I were standing there waiting and watching, but she wouldn't look at us. I couldn't blame her after all she had been through these past couple of weeks.

Chapter 15
Terriana

I could feel their eyes on me, but I just couldn't bring myself to invite them inside. Jess lied to me. She never even told me he came looking for me; maybe I could have changed him. Maybe he wouldn't have done all of this, *but mom*. How could he? I thought he loved her, but I guess love has an expiration date after all. He really left me for dead too, drenched in gasoline and bound like a pig for slaughter. I meant nothing to him, less than nothing. Why were people so heartless? Why was I so hard to love? What crime did I commit that made me so undeserving of even my flesh and blood's affection?

Then there was Vinte. He invaded my senses as if he owned them. This man ignited my body with only one stare. I couldn't look at him for my own sanity. We accepted the love we thought we deserved, and I couldn't be in love with this ghost of a man who haunted my best dreams. Every time I felt scared, I would close my eyes and he would be there, fanning my ear with his breath saying '*Give in to me,*' but I couldn't. He knew me before that night at the club. He knew everything about me and pretended as if he was meeting me for the first time. I couldn't believe how juvenile I was. He lied about how he found me, to my face.

Asshole.

I felt so humiliated. I fucked him after just meeting him. I stayed the night, and we did so many things the next day, steamy, sticky, sweet things, but I couldn't give in to him.

"Terri, am sorry," I heard Jess saying from behind me, but I continued looking out the window at the clear sky. "It wasn't as if you wanted to see him. He hurt you for so many years, and he looked scary as hell when he showed up. I didn't want him hurting you again. You were finally in a good space, and you were trying to be happy. I wanted you to be happy, Terri." I think my resolve broke when I heard her voice crack, and the floodgates opened up into ugly snot-dripping tears. She hid the grandfather being CIA part too, but I wasn't mad; it saved me after all . I looked over my shoulder and patted the little space behind me, my own tears threatening to slip through. She climbed on the tiny bed and wrapped her arms around me, eventually we cried ourselves to sleep.

I could feel Jess still pressed up against me above the uncomfortable hospital sheets, but that wasn't why my eyes were still closed. I knew he stayed the night again, outside my room, all night like the heartbreaking superman that he was. To be honest, I didn't even know what I was mad about; him lying to me or him being my whole enchilada when I thought I had no one.

"Happy birthday, beautiful."

Damn, I miss him.

Just his voice had my heart crushed and my body craving for him, as if he was made to scramble all my self-control. As I opened my eyes to face my biggest weakness, I melted a little in this ungodly bed. His hair looked like he ran his fingers through it a couple hundred times. He had morning stubbles on his face, and his eyes told a million stories of dread, fear, and mostly apologetic anxiety. In his hand was a single bluebell.

"Thank you," I simply replied. I guess it was my birthday, and I didn't even know.

"I really hoped to get you something nice, but I had a feeling you wouldn't accept me wrapped in a ribbon with a big 'am sorry' on the shirt." His eyes didn't meet mine with that confession.

"I would have loved you," I whispered out, shaking on the inside for being so weak. It was like nothing clicked without him.

He took a step closer, and I just wanted to hold him. He had a tortured look on his face that I just wanted to kiss away. My emotions were so fucking contradictory. "I wanted to meet you so badly; the girl whose walk made my breath hitch, the girl with that heart-wrenching smile. I wanted to meet you, and I should have told you but how? I didn't want to endanger you. For the job I can't go around telling people where I work. I just wanted to meet you," he explained. The evident pain in his voice was hurting my nerves a little.

"He found me through you," I replied, completely aware of how wrong I was to put this on him.

He looked down with a deep sigh. "Am sorry, Terri. I fought with myself for months trying to kill the desire I unwillingly harnessed for you. Then when I saw you at the club, it was like faith. I can't stop thinking about you. All I want is a redo. You're it for me." His breath was shaky yet so sincere, but so was my father's words once upon a time.

They are not the same, and you know it.

Why was I fighting this, *him?*

162

"I can't," I choked out.

"You just need a little time. You've been through a lot," he said to me, peering through my soul in the process like he could see the girl still tied to a post in the back of my mind. "I think I fell in love with you on that dance floor," he said, shattering my heart with the words of a saint.

"People say that love is endless, so please wait for me, because… I think I love you too." It was almost a whisper when the words left my lips.

"You need a little time, and that's okay with me. You're trying to heal, and am rooting for you, for us," he said hopefully.

"It's funny how I thought I had cut ties with him when he left me the first time, but when he left me tied to the post with the place on fire the second time." *Sigh*. "I realize it isn't as easy walking away from the ones who broke us like the ones we love." I saw a little hurt in his eyes, and I knew he understood what I meant.

"Well, as long as you love me, there's hope for us, so do what you must for now. I will wait as long as it takes. I'll wait for you to come to me. Jess can find me, if not, am finding you, and I'll never let you go. I'll be your next birthday gift. You deserve someone to stay, and it will be me." With those words he walked over and left a chaste kiss on my lips, handed me the flower, and walked out.

Epilogue
Terriana

Why was I chained to my house like a woman under house arrest? Jess has called nine times asking me the same line, "What are you going to do?" Each time I hung up after saying he was mine. So why haven't I gone to claim my man after one year? Why was Vinte's Claim holding me hostage?

Fuck it.

I threw the covers off and headed to my bathroom. I stripped bare and looked myself over. With a deep sigh, I got to work, giving myself a sphynx kitty, exfoliating my whole body, and more. I haven't felt a man's touch since his lips were on mine last. Every date has ended in "You seem far away right now, Terri. I thought you wanted to come out with me tonight?" But that was only half of it. I wanted him out of my mind, but no one else existed other than him. Their touch made my insides turn, and all I wanted was Vinte to turn my insides out.

I bit my lip just thinking about how massive he was; either that or I was just inexperienced. As I finished beautifying and showering, I combed my hair and began

165

strolling through racks in my closet. I needed to look hot, *no, fierce, ahh*. Once I didn't look as broken as I felt trying to find myself this past year.

I got cute in a black sleeveless corset, some yellow flowing high-waist pants, and my lucky heels. I got a clutch and dabbed on some make-up, a splash of cologne, followed by some shea butter lotion, and I did a once over in the mirror. "You're gorgeous, and he's yours, queen." I had been singing this stupid mantra since Jess had coffee with him, and he apparently said he belonged to me. To some, that would be stalker material, but to me, I have been wet just thinking about him saying it.

I made my way to my front door and swung it open. Before I could step out, my heart stopped. The most beautiful hazel eyes stared back at me, black jeans, black "V" neck shirt and a badass leather jacket with the cockiest grin, and a single bluebell in hand.

Déjà vu?

"I thought about getting a ribbon, but I only want to unwrap you," he sighed out, raking his eyes over me, ravishing every inch of me, and he hadn't even touched me yet.

"Vinte," I breathe out shakily. I was on my way to claim him once and for all, so why was I still frozen as stiff as a fucking board.

166